Swiss Mistletoe and Macarons

by

Amey Zeigler

Christmas Cookies Series

Swiss Mistletoe and Macarons

COPYRIGHT © 2021 by Amey Zeigler

Cover Art by *Tina Lynn Stout*

The Wild Rose Press, Inc.
PO Box 708
Adams Basin, NY 14410-0708
Visit us at www.thewildrosepress.com

Publishing History
First Edition, 2021
Digital ISBN 978-1-5092-3926-9

Christmas Cookies Series
Published in the United States of America

She was cute in her plum-colored sweater and jeans. She was American pie, not sophisticated *crème brulée*.

She smirked. "And I thought you noticed my accent."

"I did...amongst other things." He looked at her clothes, then back to her face. "Friend of the American bride, I take it?" He nodded toward Lainey, the bride-to-be greeting friends in the corner.

"Actually, the groom. Yves is my cousin."

Jean-Marc raised his brows. Yves was an old school-mate who grew up in Vevey. "Ah, yes, his mother is American."

She dipped her chin in a nod. "My mother's sister."

Before she recounted her genealogy, Jean-Marc searched for a different subject. "You seem to have discriminating taste. What do you think of our little preparations?" He held out a hand toward the table spread with his and Alexandre's work of more than three days.

"Your *petit fours* are passable but a little soggy." She pinched the air. "Either you used too much sugar glaze, or you let your fillings soak through the cake." She curled her lip. "Quite frankly, I expected better."

Soggy? Did she know who he was? Anyone who knew anything about pastries either knew of his show or his cook books. "I am Jean-Marc Dobrinsky. Perhaps you've heard of me. I have a show, *Passionate Pastries*, on a popular streaming channel."

She jutted out her chin. "Never heard of it."

Dedication

To my brother Marc, a fabulous storyteller in his own right.

Chapter 1

Jean-Marc Dobrinsky drummed his thumbs across his knees. Everything he'd worked toward for the last seven years would hopefully pay off after this pitch meeting with the great producer-chef Jacques Thisset.

Several people—all no doubt waiting to see the famous chef himself—sat in the black and metal chairs—the same kind which bit into the center of Jean-Marc's back. Inhaling, he calmed his heart. He only had to go into Thisset's London office, project confidence, and ask the production company for hundreds of thousands of pounds to take his show off his private, online streaming service and produce his show for the masses.

Stilling his jittering leg, Jean-Marc sighed. Jacques Thisset was the greatest of the great. Like Jean-Marc, Thisset started as a dishwasher—only Thisset began in one of the top restaurants in Paris, not London—and worked his way up the ladder as he studied culinary arts in the best French schools. After years of starring in England's most popular culinary television series, he moved to producing. Now he would judge if Jean-Marc had the chops to star in his own British TV show. Would Jean-Marc's years of videoing and editing his own show pay off with this interview?

A woman, clad all in gray, propped open the door. She consulted a tablet. "Jean-Marc Dobrinsky?"

Hearing his name, he grabbed his wool peacoat and stood. Towering above her, he nodded to the woman and followed her through the doorway. His throat squeezed shut. Would Jacques Thisset conduct the interview in his native French, or would they speak English? Jean-Marc's English was great, but it was not his mother's tongue. Growing up in Switzerland, he spoke little of his father's Polish and learned French from his Swiss mother before she left his father and him when he was five. After he moved to England ten years ago, he learned English as a way to share his pastry tips in his videos. His accent was unmistakable, and his vocabulary still lacked essential words.

Jacques Thisset sat at a desk in his office.

A bookcase stuffed with awards from both Thisset's culinary show and culinary arts intimidated Jean-Marc. To his left, a window cut from the beige wall showed the gray, winter skies of London's business district.

Thisset smiled.

Age claimed most of his hair. Patches of white still clung, like Chantilly cream, to the fringes of his shining bald head. A white mustache filled in the space between his nose and his lip. Like Jean-Marc's father, Thisset had a round, barrel chest. Jean-Marc could almost imagine him in a chef's toque and whites.

He waved a beckoning hand.

Jean-Marc's heart thundered in his chest. Meeting an idol weakened his knees. Should he greet him with the traditional French greeting of a kiss on each cheek?

Thisset leaned over the desk and shook his hand— a traditional British greeting—and motioned to the chair. "Welcome, Jean-Marc. I have heard a lot about you."

Mince! Thisset spoke in English.

Another back-biting chair sat across from the desk. Jean-Marc slipped into it.

"I've watched your show."

A zing went through Jean-Marc. *The* Jacques Thisset watched his show? "And what did you think?" He swept trembling hands over his lips.

"You could do better." Jacques lifted his chin.

So cryptic. Jean-Marc's smile faltered. A bit of wind went out of his chest. He gained over two million views on his internet show.

As he studied his tablet, Thisset rolled his finger and thumb. "Even though I have it right here, tell me your proposal. What do you envision?"

"I see, me"—Jean-Marc placed both hands on his chest—"in a professional kitchen, being my charming self and teaching the fine details of the art of pastry-making."

"Just you, eh?" Thisset furrowed his brow. "You studied at a good school."

Jean-Marc sat straighter. Thisset seemed displeased. "Yes, of course. The best."

Dropping the tablet, Thisset leaned back and crossed his hands over his dark suit. "What is your goal here with our family?"

Jean-Marc grinned. "I want your job."

Thisset raised his graying eyebrows. "You have gutsy ambition."

Was that a good thing or a bad thing? With thundering heart, Jean-Marc leaned forward, placing his hands on the armrests. "You are an example to all of us who start with a culinary certificate. You have reached the highest pinnacle of success. I desire to be your equal. I want a show as successful as yours and maybe someday produce my own."

Thisset furrowed his eyebrows. "You have no idea what it took to get here."

Jean-Marc thrust out his chin. "I have some idea." Then he held his breath and waited for the older man's response. Was he too bold? Was he too strong? Maybe Thisset thought him too egotistical.

Thisset's deep wrinkles broke into a grin. "You are that confident, are you?"

"I am."

Thisset leaned back and clasped his hands over his barrel chest. "You're young. Less than thirty, I'd guess."

Just shy of twenty-eight. Jean-Marc nodded.

With a great groaning of his chair, Thisset leaned forward. "I agreed to this interview as a favor to your father. We'll sign your show, but we require a few stipulations which will be handled by my assistant producers." He pushed a button on the intercom on his desk. "Bertha. Standard contract."

"Thank you, sir." That was it? The pitch was over? Thisset wanted his show? Electricity sprang through his chest. He wanted to embrace him. He reached out his hand.

Thisset squinted. Instead of shaking Jean-Marc's hand, Thisset bent his head over his desk, stroking his bald head and staring out the window. At last, he made eye contact. "Beware, Jean-Marc. Being famous is a lonely lifestyle. You'll have to choose your friends and associates wisely. You can only be with people who either don't know who you are or who are at least as famous. As a young man, do you really want a lifestyle in the limelight?"

Jean-Marc swallowed hard. He wanted this worldwide show more than anything else. Didn't he? What did he care for friends? "Thank you for the advice, but I have no plans for relationships at the moment."

"Too bad." He shuffled two folders on his desk. "Now might be your last chance."

Jean-Marc's chest burned. Did he say the wrong thing?

The door clicked behind him. Jean-Marc turned.

The woman in gray entered. "This way, Mr. Dobrinsky." Once in the hall, she marched to a conference room with large windows to his right. She gestured toward a seat across from her. "Now, Mr. Thisset has some stipulations." She slid the paper across the table.

He sat, read over the legally binding words, and signed the stack of papers in front of him. "Anything."

Standing near him, Bertha dug her hands into her hips. "Your streamed shows have a few flaws."

He raised his head, not even hiding his shock. "Such as?" Was his diction unclear? Would he need to take elocution lessons? Bending, he worked his way through the papers.

"You need a consistent partner."

Her words slammed into his chest. Dropping his pen, Jean-Marc raised his eyebrows. He'd worked with so many disappointing people. "A partner? I pitched the show as a solo act?"

Bertha slid up her glasses higher on her nose. "In our market research analysis, we've found two people on a show create a more dynamic viewer experience. You need to find someone with chemistry, knowledge, and viewer appeal. Or we can assign you a partner."

He jumped out of his chair. Working with someone he didn't know would be *penible*—horrible! "I would prefer to find someone myself."

She clicked a pen. "Someone you've worked with in the past?"

He huffed. In the last four years of his online show, he'd worked with half a dozen or so women. None of them satisfied him as someone he wanted to stake his whole career on.

She pointed with her pen. "What about the last woman?"

He just fired the last "chef" he worked with. He wiped his hand down his face. "Kathleen doesn't know the difference between a *profiterole* and a *palmier*." He pinched the air. "The art of pastry requires exactness, and she was sloppy."

"Anyone else?"

He faced the windows showcasing London's cityscape. From here, it didn't seem so bustling. "Melanie could cook just fine..." He didn't want to admit why he found her so objectionable.

"But you didn't find her attractive."

In the reflection, he noticed her head dip and a frown paste on her brow. He spun and squinted against Bertha's frankness. "Attraction had nothing to do with her lack of skills." He shrugged. But what Bertha said was true. Melanie wasn't pleasant to the eyes.

"What about Hazel?"

She indeed followed his show. "She wanted to run the show. I need a partner, not a boss."

Bertha raised her eyebrows. "And Tanya?"

He paced. "No spark for show business. And she was bland on camera. Everyone said so. Didn't you read the comments?"

Bertha nodded. "How about Rachelle?"

"She left to have a baby, remember? That was not my fault." He raised a hand to mark his innocence.

"Nicole?"

He studied the green industrial carpet. "Nicole was beautiful and fun to work with in the kitchen, but, alas, her fiancé objected to her career choice both in the kitchen and in the public eye."

"And Penelope?"

A sting rushed through him. He sighed. Penelope had been great. They shared chemistry, and she possessed a great aptitude for the art. He dug his toe into the carpet. Penelope was gone. He faced Bertha and shook his head. He had no words.

She squinted. "By yourself, you are too bland. You need someone who complements you and who makes this show fun. Your good looks and skill can only take you so far. Our first taping starts the twenty-seventh. You must notify me of your choice of co-host for the show by Christmas."

Raising his eyebrows, he grasped his stomach. "That's in two weeks. I promised my father I'd return to Switzerland for the holidays." He also needed to announce his last streaming video. He hoped having the London producer would spare him from having to work with yet another woman who didn't live up to his expectations.

She knitted her brows. "If you don't fulfill your obligations, we will cancel your contract."

"I haven't been home for Christmas in four years. Being home this time of year means so much to my father and his faith." A sinking feeling, like a failed soufflé, filled his stomach. Plus, his father asked him to help with an engagement party for one of his friends.

She shrugged. "Maybe you can ask new graduates from your school."

He stared out the window. "I'll think of something."

"And Mr. Thisset wants an exciting *macaron* recipe so you or your new partner needs to develop something. Nothing boring. Create, Jean-Marc. Make Mr. Thisset happy. See you the twenty-seventh."

He plucked up his jacket. A dull ache pulsed in the back of his head. "Don't worry." Where would he find a woman who had chemistry and skills? He must go to his school.

****

After cooking and cleaning up after dinner, brushing the Gordons' kids' teeth, and giving one-year-old Alice a bath, Livi Hanson tucked five-year old Henry in his bed, and Alice in hers. She closed the door, making as little sound as possible.

Then she tiptoed down the hall to the Gordons' newly renovated kitchen. Boston's chill blew across the wood floors and froze her toes. Once she turned on the oven, she'd have this kitchen toasty.

With a flick of her wrist, she stuck in her earbuds, pushed Mrs. Gordon's "indoor stylist's" Christmas decor from the granite island, and pressed Play on her laptop.

Jean-Marc's show logo, Passionate Pastries, flickered on the screen.

With Mrs. Gordon's permission, Livi was allowed to watch his show in the kitchen after her nightly duties. She bought and labeled her own supplies for making pastries and kept them in a special place in the spacious pantry. As long as she did not feed the organic-raised kids her homemade pastries, she was allowed to experiment. Mrs. Gordon frowned upon her kids eating sugar. And she didn't like frowning as it caused wrinkles.

Livi clasped her hands. Electric currents thrilled through her. She found his latest video online, swept up her curly hair in a ponytail while his intro played, and wrapped her apron around herself during his advertisements.

Finally, he was on.

Interesting. He was alone again. He must've fired the new girl, Kathleen.

Livi shook her head. That man couldn't keep a woman on his show to save his life. Talented though he was, he sure failed at something if no one wanted to work with him. Yes, he was indeed eye-candy. But his charming good looks were not the reasons Livi watched his show. She was a serious student of pastries. She even bought one of his cookbooks with step-by-step illustrated instructions and a large, color picture of Jean-Marc grinning on the front cover. Sadly, no matter how hard she tried, her *macarons* always failed. Either too dry or too sticky. The Italian meringue just never looked right. She needed to find a simpler recipe.

She leaned closer with her hand on her chin, hovering over the granite to watch. The Polish-Swiss baker moved across the screen and flashed a dazzling smile. Other girls probably fell for that dimple to the left of his luscious lips, but not Livi.

He brushed a hand across his unshaved cheeks. His sleeves were rolled up to three-quarters to expose muscular forearms.

His chef coat must've been tailored to fit his slim waist and broad shoulders because he didn't look like a big white block.

He stood in front of a stainless steel counter. Behind him, white subway tile lined the wall. "After the demonstration, stay tuned. I will have a special announcement."

Livi shrugged. Whatever could it be?

Now came the part of the show she anticipated. For all of December, he showcased Christmas desserts. On the menu tonight? She held her breath. Liking to be surprised, she never read the titles or the comments until the end.

"Today I have a special treat."

His French accent added to his aesthetic.

"Here are your equipment and ingredients." A list of ingredients popped up on the screen. "Make sure you have everything ready if you want to follow along. *Mise en place.*"

"Hold on there, buster." She hit Pause to retrieve the ingredients and measured the sugar and flour with her digital scale. French pastries were so precise. She dragged out her stash from the pantry: a small saucepan, a thermometer, a strainer, a bowl, her pastry brush, parchment paper, a jelly roll pan, a whisk, and a mixer. Other than sending money to her sister, Wendy, at the University of Notre Dame, Livi only spent money on baking supplies. Her clothes? Bought ten years ago. Her hair style? A simple pony whipped around her head. She lived to bake.

When she had everything laid out in *mise en place*, she pushed Play again. "Oh, do tell. Butter, cake flour, cornstarch, eggs, sugar, and vanilla? Sounds like everything else you do in the kitchen, Jean-Marc. What makes today's choice so special?"

"You want to know what makes today's dessert special, do you?" He held out his hands and spoke through the camera.

"Of course I do." She didn't miss Kathleen, or whatever her name was, one bit.

He opened his hands across the bowl. "Today we will learn how to make a *génoise*. Once you learn how to make this foundational recipe, you can use it for many more desserts. The light and fluffy sponge will be the base for our *roulade*. Or…" He slapped the metallic countertop. "*Bûche de Noël*."

Livi caught her breath. Nothing said Christmas more than a Yule log. She licked her lips and imagined a soft cake rolled around creamy filling and decorated to look like a tree limb.

He leaned toward the camera. "Christmas for me without this delightful, light, moist, and buttery dessert would be no holiday. I learned how to make this from my father as a traditional treat where I grew up, so it is very special to me. We will add our own twist. As I always say, though pastries have been made for hundreds of years, one can always come up with a new way to prepare or present them."

Jean-Marc said that every episode. Indeed, what he said was true. Inventing a new flavoring or a new way to present it was what Livi loved the most. Jean-Marc struggled with his creativity, perhaps, always focusing on the mathematics and scientific ratios for creating instead. His partners were the creative ones. Yet, they never lasted long.

Without facing away from the camera, Jean-Marc gathered the ingredients. He placed the butter into the saucepan and lit the heat. "Boil the butter. Watch out for the water. It makes a hissing sound."

"Yes, it does." A pop of hot butter burned her hand. "Ouch!"

"Don't worry. After a while the sound will stop." He laughed.

Livi rubbed the pain on her hand. "I don't know why you don't use a microwave."

"You can't use a microwave for this step because we are separating protein solids from the water. Skim off the solids with a spoon. Don't let it burn. If you burn it, you have to start all over again." He wagged a finger.

She skimmed off the excess.

"Now you have clarified butter."

Her shoulders slumped. "Can't I just buy clarified butter? Seems easier than scalding myself." She could find that type of butter easily in any of the food stores here in Boston.

"Or you can buy ghee from the store."

"Now you tell me." With the back of her wrist, she brushed a hair from her face. "I have a jar of ghee in the fridge." She worked through the rest of the recipe. With a spatula, she spread the batter less than an inch deep into the lined pan. At last, she slipped the prepared jelly roll pan into the preheated oven. Now she had seven minutes to clean up.

After washing the dishes, she watched him make a

cream for the middle. She knew how to do that and didn't need a step-by-step tutorial. She wanted to get to the announcement. Heavenly aromas wafted from the oven. She opened the oven door. The sponge was slightly browned but not crisp. Perfect. She removed the cake and set it on the counter to cool.

The front door opened.

With a quickening heartbeat, Livi hastened to put away her last bowl. Someone was home early.

"Olivia, do you have a minute?"

Livi paused the streaming service. She would listen to Jean-Marc's announcement later. With her earbuds in, she hadn't heard Mrs. Gordon enter the kitchen. Normally she went right to bed. Dressed in a dark pant suit, and a chunky gold necklace, Mrs. Gordon looked the part of a psychologist to the rich and famous. Dark circles haunted her eyes. Her high heels clacked on the wood floor. "Yes." Livi's heart thundered. Had she forgotten to buy organic hemp milk or to take out the trash again? Mrs. Gordon's quick temper made those instances difficult to forget.

"Mr. Gordon and I would like to speak to you, if you could join us in the dining room." Mrs. Gordon disappeared from the doorframe.

"Uh, sure." She slid the earbuds from her ears. A burning filled her chest. Were they going to dismiss her? Talking to both of them didn't happen very often.

Chapter 2

London's wintery skies weighed on Jean-Marc. Gray clouds hung low, and the naked trees seemed cheerless. May was the best time to be in London, when the grass grew thick and green, and the trees displayed their fullest canopy. At least in winter, fewer tourists lined the streets taking pictures of bridges and buildings—and of himself.

He stuffed his hands in his jacket pockets and made his way toward the *École des Pâtes*. Ducking his head, he avoided stares from all the people who watched his show. While in London, more than once he was mobbed by women asking for autographs or wanting baking tips. Maybe that was why he struggled to find a woman in his personal life. Perhaps he was leery of women pawing after him because he was famous.

Swinging open the wide, glass doors, Jean-Marc nodded at the receptionist.

She smiled and waved him through.

High ceilings with smooth horizontal wood paneling surrounded the receptionist's desk. Sunlight from the large, street-side windows reflected off the gleaming, polished floor. Stairs off to the right headed to the classrooms and practice kitchens. Somewhere in the building someone baked brioche perhaps. The air hung heavy with sweetbread and sugar.

At his office door, Arnold waved him in.

Jean-Marc embraced his old master. "Thank you for taking time to meet with me, my friend."

"My pleasure. What can I do for you?"

Wrinkles lined his skin like baked *mille feuille*. From the office window, Jean-Marc studied the Thames snaking around the buildings. Big Ben towered in the distance. Jean-Marc sighed and took the seat in front of Arnold's desk. "I was offered a contract to produce my show."

"Congratulations." A huge grin spread across Arnold's face.

"Thank you." Jean-Marc gave a short nod. "The only problem is I need an on-screen partner."

Arnold raised his eyebrows. "And you are wondering if anyone graduating this winter would be interested?"

Jean-Marc hid his embarrassment of asking for a novice, but he had little choice. He dipped his chin. "Yes."

Pitching his fingers together, Arnold shook his head. "You have earned yourself quite a reputation here. No one wants to work with you. Not one person wants to be told they are not as good as the legendary Jean-Marc Dobrinsky."

Jean-Marc huffed. Maybe he allowed his ego to taint his reputation. Heat flamed his face.

Arnold sighed. "I wish I would help you, my friend. You were—are—the best—the brightest in the industry. But you will have to look elsewhere."

Jean-Marc clenched his teeth. "I need an assistant." He hoped he kept the desperation out of his voice. If the production company chose his partner, he'd lose control. His show would be over before it began.

Arnold leaned forward and wagged his pointer finger. "See? I discovered your problem. You are not searching for an equal. You are looking for someone to boss around—an assistant. Before you said you needed a partner. Which do you need, Jean-Marc—someone to fluff your ego or someone who complements you?"

Now Jean-Marc's chest burned as hot as a bread oven.

"Doesn't your father have connections in Switzerland?" Arnold leaned back, his leather chair squeaking.

"I haven't asked him." Jean-Marc sighed. He fiddled with the candy thermometer he always kept in his shoulder pocket of his chef's jacket.

"That should be your next move." Dipping his chin, Arnold bobbed his head. He stood and stretched out his hands. "Good luck."

"Thank you." Standing, Jean-Marc embraced him before stepping out and downstairs into the cold air. A dark cloud hung over him. His trip home would be busy. His father demanded his best efforts for this party. How could he focus on anything until he found a person equal to the task?

Hanging his head, he shuffled to the Tube. Perhaps by some miracle, he could find a capable pastry chef in Switzerland.

****

With dread clawing at her throat, Livi padded across the wood floors to the formal dining room. Christmas greenery swirled every object. Crystals resembling snowflakes hung from the wooden staircase banister. Snowflakes must've been the motif for this year, because they were everywhere—on top of the custom kitchen cabinets, over the Federalist-style mantle, as placemats under the pre-set dinner table, and hanging from candles in the center piece. Ugh. Most of them were glass and incredibly fragile. Still, snowflakes were better than last year's pinecones. Whenever his mom's back was turned, four-year old Henry chucked those around the room.

Mrs. Gordon took up her usual spot near the liquor cart parked in the corner. She palmed the crystal stopper for the imported Scottish whisky.

Mr. Gordon sat at the highly polished table. Deep bags under his eyes told the story of late nights and long hours at his Boston law office. His graying temples gleamed in the dim lighting. Livi's heartbeat quickened. She didn't get summoned often to speak with Mr. Gordon. She'd only met him a few times in the three years she'd worked for them. Was she too lax with the children? Her sweetheart pajamas suddenly felt out of place. She tried to read his expression, but it was the same as always—stressed.

"Do you have a passport?" He leaned forward with his eyebrows drawn.

He probably used the same expression when cross-examining his witnesses. Holding her breath, she rolled the hem of her sleeve between her fingers. "Yes." She got one last year in hopes of attending the culinary school in Paris. Sadly, it never traveled out of her bedroom drawer.

He sat back. "Livi, we have a proposal."

"Okay." She gulped. She always wondered if they were international drug smugglers. Now they had gotten caught, and they wanted to flee across the border to Canada. No wonder they had so much money.

He cleared his throat. "We plan to take the kids to Switzerland to learn how to ski for two weeks over the holidays. Normally, we give you the week off between Christmas and New Year's, but our trip will start the week before Christmas." Mr. Gordon slipped a packet of papers from his briefcase.

Wind rushed out of the room. Livi couldn't breathe. She usually had one week off from nannying at Christmas to see her sister in Indiana. Maybe she would get two weeks off! A slight grin parted her lips.

Mr. Gordon held out a contract. "We hope you will accompany us to take care of the children while we are on the slopes, when we want to go out, and at other convenient times. Here is the schedule, along with a written agreement."

Livi took the contract—a legally binding and extremely lengthy contract. The words blurred on the page. Livi blinked back tears. No Christmas vacation? No time with her sister? No time for Christmas baking? No Christmas traditions? And one less week to drop off all the cookies to all the neighbors. This unexpected overtime threw a wrench into all her Christmas plans. Convenient times for them, he meant, but not for her.

Mrs. Gordon took another gulp from the tumbler. "Naturally, we've already scheduled your time off. We would compensate you for any arrangements you have already made. We would also pay you time and a half while you are with us, including but not limited to the whole two weeks."

The extra money would be nice. She could use it to go toward her pastry school tuition. "What would my schedule be like?" Would she have time to go to Paris? Or see other cities in Europe?

He nodded toward the paper. "I've included a calendar as Addendum E."

She flipped to the back. In a bold grid, Mr. Gordon scheduled everything. *Tuesday morning: family breakfast on the balcony. Wednesday evening: fondue at the lodge. Friday night: couple time.* And on and on. Each activity was color coordinated. A star at the bottom gave her the key. Blue was when she was to be with the family. Red was when they wanted to be alone. Her times off were sporadic—an afternoon here, a morning there, and only four free evenings. He was thorough.

Her heart sank. Not enough time to travel anywhere.

"We gave you Christmas Eve and Christmas morning and a few times when we'd want some exclusive family time on the slopes or at the lodgings. But we rented a three-hundred-year-old traditional, yet fully renovated, Swiss chalet with a heated indoor pool."

"Of course." But she'd be alone on Christmas. Where could she possibly go for Christmas Eve except her room? What joy and gladness would be found there? The three-hundred-year-old chalet better have lightning-fast Wi-Fi.

Mr. Gordon pointed to the clump of papers. "I detailed it all in a contract as an addendum to your regular scheduled services here. We'll cover food, board, flight, and lodging. But the stipulation of no boyfriends still applies."

Not that Livi minded. The last time she had a date was a year ago with the guy who worked at the French pastry shop on the corner. And she totally understood the clause. Mrs. Gordon came home one night and found the last nanny in the master suite with her boyfriend. At least the nanny's boyfriend wasn't Mr. Gordon.

Mrs. Gordon leaned against her husband's chair. She'd gulped several full tumblers already.

"Read it over and let us know within twenty-four hours so that we know what to plan on."

Livi nodded. Mr. Gordon loved his deadlines.

"We know this trip will be a sacrifice for you, as it is last minute. We've added a little extra bonus, as well, for the inconvenience."

She glanced at the sum. Her eyebrows rose. "Thank you. That's generous." She tucked the papers under her arm and headed back to the kitchen. Her sponge had cooled. It hardened in the pan. Instead of a *roulade*, she'd have to settle for a layered cake. She shrugged and wiped a hand down her face. All that time wasted. No, not wasted. She learned a new skill she could repeat in the future.

How did she feel about going to Switzerland for Christmas? Didn't cousin Yves live in Switzerland? Or was it Sweden? She pulled out her phone from her pocket and sent him a text. In the meantime, what to do about Christmas?

Maybe she should call Wendy. She dialed her number. "Hey, Wendy."

"I was about to call you. I have bad news. I had to put about four thousand dollars on my credit card."

"What?" Tension in her neck throbbed.

"My car died, and it needed repairs. I don't have any money to pay it off. And without the car I can't get to class and buy food."

Four thousand dollars? Livi's throat tightened. How could she pay that bill? What would Mom do if she were here? "Fine. I'll send you half."

"But I don't have the other two grand. This is my last semester before I graduate."

A bead of guilt bubbled up in her heart. Who else would help Wendy? "Fine. I'll send you the whole four thousand." There went her entire bonus for working over Christmas. Now she had to go to Switzerland. Just when she thought might get ahead financially, something always came up. She sighed. "I won't be returning home for Christmas, though."

"Why not?"

A deep haunting sunk her. "The Gordons asked me to accompany them to Switzerland for the holiday. They're going skiing."

"That's so not fair."

Livi agreed. Sometimes the Gordons asked too much.

"You always get to do the fun things. I wish I could go."

Huffing, Livi raised her eyebrows. "It's not fair that I get to go? Or it's not fair the Gordons asked me to sacrifice my winter break? This trip isn't a vacation. I'll be watching the kids the whole time." She lowered her voice to make sure her employers didn't hear.

"Yes, but it's still a trip to Europe. And Switzerland! And I have to stay here and study."

Wendy sounded as though she had thrown herself on her bed. Livi shook her head. "Someday when I'm a famous chef, I will take you to Europe, and we can travel all around. I promise."

"Like that will ever happen. Be sure to bring me

back something—a watch or some chocolate."

A beeping sound buzzed in Livi's ear. "Wendy, I've got to go. Yves is on the other line."

"Fine. I hope you have a miserable time and break a leg skiing."

Wendy still used her manipulative tricks. Livi exhaled. "The kids are going skiing. Not me."

"Then I hope you get frostbite. Kidding!"

Rolling her eyes, Livi sighed at her little sister's tantrum. "Bye, Wendy." She clicked the button to switch calls. "Hello! Sorry I texted you at six a.m. your time. I am coming to Switzerland in two weeks."

"That's wonderful!"

Yves's tenor voice rang in the phone. Livi missed his French accent.

"You'll be here in time to meet Lainey and come to our engagement party."

"I'd love to!" Livi raised her eyebrows. Yves focused so much on his career, she never thought he'd marry.

"You'll have to text me when you get into town, and I'll send you the details."

At least seeing her cousin and attending his engagement party took a little sting out of not being at home for Christmas. When she quit the call, she felt a pit form in her stomach. How could she even enjoy her Christmas this year?

Chapter 3

After one week of crazy preparations, Livi stepped foot for the first time on foreign soil. The flight from Boston to Geneva wore her out.

Henry hit the bathroom every five minutes with the excitement of being on a real plane.

Livi paced up and down the aisle in coach with Alice in order to put her to sleep. At nearly one year, Alice weighed a ton on Livi's shoulder. Livi hoped their parents enjoyed their eye masks, aromatic food, and sleeper beds in first class. Without any hope of sleeping, she stuck in an ear bud and listened to a few episodes of a TV series while Alice nestled into her neck. Her breath smelled of milk.

Henry snuggled his head on Livi's lap.

She stroked Henry's baby-fine hair away from his face. Tender moments of quiet with the kids melted Livi's heart.

Dawn broke, and light splashed through the cabin windows. The plane safely landed in snow-covered Geneva.

Livi squeezed between two car seats in the back of a black SUV. But she didn't mind. The view stirred her. Geneva had a similar feel to Boston—old, crowded, and snowy. A white skiff covered the gray mansard roofs topping the rows of limestone buildings surrounding the lake. But the closeness of the mountains amazed her.

She couldn't appreciate the full effect. The clouds clung to the snow-heavy peaks, obscuring their height. But even seeing just the bases of the mountains thrilled her.

Out of the city, snow dusted the tiered vineyards cut into the sides of the hills. Sun broke through the clouds with beams of light, illuminating Lake Geneva. At Vevey, they headed deeper into the mountains.

"I'm glad we rented the four-wheel drive." Mr. Gordon shifted the gears.

Snow turned to brown slush on the roads. Everything became a blur of white.

Mrs. Gordon's phone gave directions every so often.

With the heat blowing on her, Livi dozed. When the car stopped, she woke.

"This is it." Mrs. Gordon propped open the door.

With blurred eyes, Livi peered through the icy windshield.

A wooden chalet sat on the edge of a mountain. Ornamental wood covered the top half. Wooden cutout beams supported the pitched roof. Carvings of a compass rose, flowers, and curves decorated every inch of the wood.

"It looks small." Mrs. Gordon stood outside in her designer boots and a huge coat.

Mr. Gordon pointed below. "Most is on the downward side of the slope."

Livi helped the kids out of the car seats and carried Alice to the front door.

Mr. Gordon had already opened it and took the first suitcases inside.

The chalet was much bigger than it appeared outside. Off to the right, a sweeping wooden staircase headed both up and downstairs. Knotted wood paneling covered all the walls and ceilings. The kitchen was small. Livi bit her lip. Hardly enough room to do any real baking. It was updated with newer appliances and hardware, but still had only a single countertop. A small oven, fridge, and stovetop were set into carved wooden cabinets.

She couldn't wait to stop at the local grocery store and buy ingredients for any baking. Here in Europe, she wouldn't need to go to specialty sections to find imported goods like vanilla sachets and butter with the right fat content to make pastries. She mentally rubbed her hands together.

Huge windows opened at the back, split only by a stacked stone fireplace reaching all the way to the thirty-foot ceilings. A cozy seating area surrounded the hearth. *Wow!* What beautiful mountains! Livi carried Alice over to look over the view. A white valley spread beneath them. In the distance, a castle rested on the hilltop. A thrill shuddered through her. Castles didn't exist in Boston.

Henry clunked down the spiral stairs one at a time.

"Livi, come look at this," he called.

Livi stepped down the stairs. The temperature dropped a little as she descended. Painted pictures of cows, black-and-white photos of snowy peaks, and the same flower motif hung along the paneled hallway. Each petal pointed outward. A cluster of seeds remained in the middle. What flower was this? She read the little print on the bottom. *Edelweiss.*

Off to the side, she noticed a room with only one bed. She peeked inside. A black silhouette of cows traversing a mountain was painted on the door leading to a private bath. A small window lit the room. This was her sleeping quarters, she was sure. Definitely livable for the next two weeks. She found a wooden-framed mirror over a small dresser and showed Alice herself. "This will be fun, won't it?"

Alice smiled at her reflection. Two front teeth glowed in her little mouth.

"I found the pool!"

With jolt of alarm sending energy to her heart, Livi followed Henry's voice to the end of the hall. She didn't want him throwing himself in without someone to watch him.

The temperature turned moist and warm once she found Henry. In the center of the room, a glistening pool reflected another wall of windows opened to the reflective light coming off the snow outside. On the opposite wall was another silhouette of little girls and little boys walking with cows—not what she would consider the height of sophistication, but very charming. Everywhere she turned were reminders she was in Switzerland—in the paintings, decor, and the white cross in the middle of red symbolizing their flag. Also on the wall hung the white and black flag of the canton of Fribourg.

"Come on, Henry. Let's go help your mom and dad bring in the luggage." Livi held out her hand and tugged him up the spiral staircase. She only had a few hours to get unloaded, unpacked, situated, and to get down to Vevey that night for the engagement party. She reached the kitchen.

Mr. Gordon stood near the island. "You won't mind tending the kids, would you? Margie has a headache, and I could really use a nap."

A nap? Her heart sank. "According to the schedule, I was supposed to have the night off. I made other plans to see family in Vevey."

Taking out some Swiss *francs*, he waved them. "If you won't mind taking the kids, I will drive you down there. You can also pick up a treat."

"Sure." Just what she wanted—to drag a five-year-old and a toddler to an engagement party. But what else could she do? She snatched the Swiss *francs* with a frown. She was at their mercy.

****

Jean-Marc had been on his feet since four a.m. He whipped and baked in his father's kitchen at the Grand Hotel de Vevey in Switzerland. The menu was seven pages long with *vol-au-vents*, savory pastries, veggies, and an even longer list of sweet pastries. One would think he was catering for a king. And his father wanted Jean-Marc to make his rosettes. Pastry wrapped into roses and soaked in red wine, which he prepared days ago. Now he had to fry them.

His father filled the kitchen with impressive presence. He worked around the countertop efficiently and with exactness. His rotund figure in a white chef's coat never stopped for a moment.

Alexandre Dobrinsky wiped a wrist across his brow. "We have so much work to do—so many preparations. Everything has to be perfect for Lainey and Yves."

"Of course." When Jean-Marc got into the zone, everything disappeared. He loved being in the kitchen with his father and creating, but today he was distracted. With great care, he dipped each rolled ribbon of pastry rosette into the heated oil.

"Is something bothering you, my son?"

Jean-Marc hadn't realized he sounded distant. He hadn't realized how much the contract weighed on him. "I signed the contract for my new show."

Alexandre stopped hulling strawberries. "It's official?"

His father's French was still heavily accented. As a child, Jean-Marc was embarrassed by his father's accent. Now he was proud of his Polish heritage. "We start taping on the twenty-seventh."

Alexandre first spoke in Polish. His words poured out in a jumble. He grabbed Jean-Marc by both shoulders and kissed both cheeks. "*Félicitations*! You have worked hard to be here. No one is better at pastries than you."

The compliment stung. Heat broiled in his chest. Being good might be part of his problem. "I have one little snag, though." He bent his head and fried more rosettes.

"What is it?" His father continued hulling strawberries for the cake.

He bit his lip. "I have to find a partner."

Alexandre shrugged and dropped more greens into a pile on the counter. "That's not so difficult."

Problem was, he'd already burned a lot of bridges with his string of firing people. No one in London wanted the job. "Do you know anyone?" His fingers smelled of the sweet wine and had a tinge of red. He wiped them on a towel and faced his father.

Alexandre raised his gaze toward the ceiling, then shook his head. "No, but what I do know is things often work themselves out. You wait and see."

Sighing, he scooped up another rosette with the

spider-catch and tapped it on the edge of the pan. Where could he find someone over Christmas? "Not this time. I have already spoken to several agencies and asked about all the graduates of the London schools. I need someone, or they will cancel the show. I need someone who speaks English."

With the huller, Alexandre dug into the greens with his massive hands. "Other pastry chefs should be jumping on such an opportunity."

Jean-Marc bit his lip. "I might have exhausted my possibilities."

"I know what your problem is." Alexandre pointed with the strawberry huller.

His face flamed. If his father brought up his ego, he would scream. "What? No, you don't."

"I caused your problem."

Alexandre placed a thick hand across his chest, covering his gold cross. Jean-Marc waved a hand and, in a colander, washed more strawberries under the water. "How could this problem be your fault?"

"I gave you my passion, my talent, and my drive for success. You grew up cooking beside me in the kitchen. How could you not but succeed?" Alexandre spread his hands wide. "You were light years ahead of your class. You grasped concepts of baking, the science of ingredients, and the flare for the artistry required to be a pastry chef, but you have taken it to a whole new level."

Jean-Marc wasn't sure if that was a compliment or not. With a tea towel, he patted the strawberries dry.

Alexandre grabbed them with both hands. "In your drive for success, you have forgotten that not everyone is a God at pastries. You were given that gift as a young child. You have certainly nourished your talent and your desire, but in your drive, you have forgotten to have patience with other people. Your instinct and intuition have been your greatest gifts, but when they are lacking in other people, you lose your temper. You expect everyone to be like you."

Jean-Marc stared at the overcast sky through the small rectangle window above the stainless steel counters. "That's not it. I just haven't found someone who is equally passionate about pastries." Alexandre laid his heavy hands on Jean-Marc's shoulders. He felt like a kid again.

"Oh, my son." He leveled his gaze. "You will have a difficult road until you learn this lesson: other people have strengths where you have weaknesses. If you cannot admit you have weakness, or that someone else has a complementary strength, your success is at an end. You can only go so far on your own. At some point, you need others."

Jean-Marc inhaled, breathing in strawberries and red wine. His father was full of advice. Only about half was worth taking. This latest bit of advice was in which half?

His father threw up his hands. "We've got lots of work to do on for this party. Lainey and Yves are important clients—no, my best clients." He studied the cake and the pile of berries on the counter. "And it looks as if we need more strawberries! *Quelle horreur*! Will you run to the *épicerie* and grab another kilo or two? We cannot run out!"

"Sure." Jean-Marc removed his apron. He'd do anything to end this conversation.

"Quickly! We only have an hour left." Alexandre

clapped his hands. "Listen, if you give yourself to serving others, things will work out. God will drop someone in your lap. You'll see."

With a hat covering his head, Jean-Marc jammed his fists into his coat he threw over his chef's jacket. The wind from the lake was bitter cold. London winters thinned his blood. He wrapped his scarf around him, covering his face up to his nose. He wished he had his father's faith.

Chapter 4

Livi's arms ached from pushing Alice's stroller up the steep stone-paved streets of Vevey. At nearly five p.m., the sun already declined behind the mountains. The sky darkened in the east. The party didn't start until six. What was she supposed to do with these kids for another hour? "Keep up, Henry."

Henry trailed behind a few feet, dragging his shoes across the Belgian block. "I'm hungry."

Their meal schedules were all messed up, and the kids suffered terrible jet lag. She wished they could all take a nap with the Gordons. Oh, well.

After an icy drive descending into Vevey, Mr. Gordon dropped her off with the kids earlier. So she strolled around the block of the Grand Hôtel de Vevey.

Livi's head throbbed from lack of sleep. Her stomach growled. Yves texted the party was catered, but she didn't know how child-friendly the food would be. She doubted everything would be sugar-free and organic.

Alice whined and turned in her seat.

Livi waited for Henry to catch up. "I'm hungry, too."

"Can we get a snack?" Henry's gloved hand snatched her sleeve.

A snack probably wouldn't hurt their whacked-out appetites, and she hated seeing them suffer. "All right."

Choosing and buying a snack would kill time and get them out of the freezing wind coming off the lake.

A small grocer's light spilled onto the sidewalk. She ducked inside the narrow entrance with Alice and Henry. Immediately the warmth of the small, cramped shop flooded her. She unzipped her jacket. Maybe she should grab some painkillers while she was there.

The small grocers only had a few aisles and next to nil in selection. At least it had the essentials—snacks and ibuprofen.

She paced the aisles. Should she pick a snack that was more filling? Or just something to tide them over? If only she knew what would be at the party. Henry hated shrimp and wouldn't eat anything green. She sighed. She would stay at the party as long as the kids behaved. If they went off the rails, she could take the bus back up to the chalet. Best grab something in between. "All right, Henry," she whispered, their footsteps the only sound in the store. "Pick out a treat. Nothing too sweet, or I'll get in trouble."

"I don't ever want to get you in trouble." He crumpled his brow at the chocolate and then at the gummies. "Can I get two?"

Henry's voice carried throughout the small store.

The grocer stared.

With a warm face, Livi put her forefinger to her lips. "Shh. Just one. Can you whisper, Henry?"

He nodded. "These are all weird." He lowered his voice. "I want my favorite. Don't they have normal candy bars?"

Alice banged a hand on the stroller tray.

Livi unbuckled her and held her on her hip. She snatched up a small box of crackers. "Remember when we got on the plane? We flew to a different country. They have different candy bars and treats here. You can discover a new favorite."

"But I want my usual candy bar." His bottom lip stuck out and curled nearly to his chin.

Arguing with a tired and cranky five-year-old was useless. Livi huffed out a laugh. His curled lip reminded her of a Swiss cake roll. She knelt beside him. "When you're in a different country, you need to get used to new and different things. But look, here are gummy bears, just like the ones we have back home. You want to try them?"

He ducked his head into his shoulders.

Starved and exhausted, Livi was about to lose her patience. She stood and rubbed her forehead.

The door opened with an icy breeze, and a man blew in. A hat hung low over his forehead, and a scarf covered the lower half of his face. His eyes were barely visible.

She moved the stroller out of his way. "You can get the gummies, or you can get a bar, but those are the two choices."

"But I don't want those!" His voice rose. Clenching his fists, Henry stamped a foot. "They're weird."

The scarf-man's head shot up, and he flicked his gaze at her.

Heat rose to her face. She ducked her head. Egad! Their English or Henry's antics must have attracted the scarf-man's attention. Either way, she needed Henry to calm down. "Shhhhh." She rubbed a hand over his shoulder to soothe him. "Gummies or chocolate?"

Henry scowled. "I don't want either." Lowering his

voice a little, he folded his arms over his jacket and moved away from her touch.

Livi inhaled. He was tired and hungry and feeling probably as bad as she, only he was five and didn't know how to handle his feelings. "Listen." She leaned over, situating Alice to off-set her weight. She rubbed the tension in her forehead. Her bed called her. Stress raked through her body. The last thing she wanted to do was argue with a five-year-old over a snack he wasn't even supposed to have. "You can have one of those, or you can wait until we get back to our chalet, but we won't get home until late tonight. The choice is yours. You'll make a good choice."

With eyebrows still furrowed, Henry plucked up a candy bar and handed it over.

"Very good. Let's pay for these and go walk along the lake, shall we?"

Henry didn't move from his spot.

Lugging a squirmy Alice, Livi pushed the stroller up to the cash desk. She placed the pain meds, the crackers for Alice, and Henry's candy bar on the counter. Her head pounded.

The cashier picked up the crackers and typed in the price.

"Wait." Henry held a bag of gummies. "I want these instead."

"Hold on," she said to the cashier, readjusting Alice on her hip. "Do you speak English? *Parlez-vous*...Never mind. Hold on." She held up a finger. "Wait a second." She stepped away with the candy bar.

The man with the scarf swooped in front of the cashier's desk and spoke to the man in French. He handed him containers of strawberries.

The cashier rang his items.

With the candy bar still in hand, Livi waved it like a banner. "Excuse me. We are checking out. I just stepped out of line to get the gummies."

Alice wailed and bonked Livi on the chin with her head.

The scarf-man shrugged. "I'm sorry. I'm in a terrible rush." The scarf muffled his words.

Livi could only see his eyes. She shifted Alice to her other hip. "The children are very hungry."

He raised an eyebrow. "So I see. But this is terribly important."

Snatching the gummies, Livi huffed. "More important than starving kids?" She was this close to flinging the candy bar in his face. Only a thread separated her from going off on him. She plopped the gummies and the candy bar on the counter next to the other purchases.

"I don't have time to explain." The man spoke to the cashier in French.

The cashier smiled and nodded.

High school French was useless for understanding anything other than slow-speaking teachers. She tapped her foot, her lips in a tight line.

The cashier bagged the man's purchases.

Alice wailed.

With all the burning anger in her heart, Livi scowled at the scarf-man.

At last, he held up his bag. "Thank you for letting me go first." He left out the door as quickly as he breezed in.

"I didn't let you. Jerk," she murmured under her breath. She dug around in her purse for her wallet and for the cash the Gordons gave her. She handed him a twenty Swiss *franc.*

The cashier held out his hand and shook his head. "*Non.*"

She held it out again. Why wouldn't he take it? Was he out of change? She just needed the items. "Please." Was he seriously not allowing her to buy the food for the starving children? Tears pricked her eyes. What a horrible country! These poor kids would go hungry for the next hour. How would she survive two whole weeks here?

The cashier pointed toward the door. "He pay." His heavily accented English was better than her French.

"What?" She dropped her jaw. "He paid for what?"

The cashier nodded to her items. "Candy. All. He already pay."

Relief spread through her. She stared out the door where scarf-man left. Guilt and gratitude mingled in her heart.

With a huge grin, Henry held the gummies and the candy bar to his chest.

"I don't think so." Livi flashed him a teasing smile. "You don't get both, Henry. Sorry. The chocolate is for me." She fed Alice a few crackers, settled her into the stroller, and pushed her out the door, zipping up her coat in the cold air. She opened the bag of gummies for Henry.

He dug into them and stuffed them into his mouth.

She opened the bar and bit into it. Chocolate coated her mouth, relaxing her. He was still a jerk. Paying for her snacks didn't absolve him of guilt. She hoped she'd never see him again.

****

The food looked perfect.

Jean-Marc surveyed the party held in the ballroom of the Grand Hôtel de Vevey. A young woman lingered near his pastries. Her hair tumbled about her shoulders in waves like ribbons of homemade caramel. Her figure had perfect curves. He switched out some platters near her. He'd seen her before, but where?

She brought a pastry to her nose. "A hint of cardamom and clove. Interesting choice."

He arched a brow. She had to be an experienced smellier to pick out those flavors. He leaned closer. "Did you try the lavender-honey baclava?"

She glanced up and then stepped back. A gasp left her lips.

He dropped his jaw. The young woman from the *épicerie*! Did she recognize him from the store? Did she recognize him from the show?

Her eyes widened. "You!" she said in English.

A pastel blush tinged her cheeks. "Me!" He couldn't help but be a little tickled at her surprise. A flash hit his stomach. "Where are your children? I hope you got them something to eat."

Then her eyes narrowed. "They are not my children. And yes, I got them something to eat." She pointed to a table where the two sat and ate. "Are you often in the habit of making hungry children wait for you?"

Not her children? He warmed inside. So she wasn't their *maman*. "I needed those strawberries for tonight." Did she even know who she was talking to? He smirked.

She thrust up her chin. "You should never be in too much of a rush to be kind."

"Don't you think my efforts paid off?" He pointed to his masterpieces. Color and texture mingled on the table. Aromas of orange, anise, and rose brushed against his nose. The strawberries—the very berries he bought at the last minute—were stacked on top of a chocolate cake.

"Your cookies are too crunchy."

She bit into one as if to prove her point. Crumbs fell from her perfect red lips. Shaking his head, he crossed his arms and studied her jeans, running trainers, and ponytail. "You must be American."

"Oh? How can you tell?" Her eyes widened. She brushed away a crumb.

He arched a brow. "Because in England *cookies* are called biscuits and are crisp."

A hint of a smile touched her lips.

She was cute in her plum-colored sweater and jeans. She was American pie, not sophisticated *crème brulée*.

She smirked. "And I thought you noticed my accent."

"I did...amongst other things." He looked at her clothes, then back to her face. "Friend of the American bride, I take it?" He nodded toward Lainey, the bride-to-be greeting friends in the corner.

"Actually the groom. Yves is my cousin."

Jean-Marc raised his brows. Yves was an old schoolmate who grew up in Vevey. "Ah, yes, his mother is American."

She dipped her chin in a nod. "My mother's sister."

Before she recounted her genealogy, Jean-Marc searched for a different subject. "You seem to have discriminating taste. What do you think of our little preparations?" He held out a hand toward the table spread with his and Alexandre's work of more than three days.

"Your *petit fours* are passable but a little soggy." She pinched the air. "Either you used too much sugar glaze, or you let your fillings soak through the cake." She curled her lip. "Quite frankly, I expected better."

Soggy? Did she know who he was? Anyone who knew anything about pastries either knew of his show or his cookbooks. "I am Jean-Marc Dobrinsky. Perhaps you've heard of me. I have a show, *Passionate Pastries*, on a popular streaming channel."

She jutted out her chin. "Never heard of it."

He narrowed his eyes. "But you do know something about pastries? I see it in your eyes. Admit it."

She shrugged. "I've learned a little. You're missing something, though." She tapped her chin.

"Me? Lacking something?" Heat rushed to his face. How dare she! If her eyes weren't the color of cocoa and her hair like spun sugar, he would've turned on his heel and left in a huff.

" 'Pastries have been made for hundreds of years, but one can always find a new way to prepare or present them.' And you have failed to present these in an interesting manner."

He dropped his jaw. "That's my line. You *have* watched my show!" A thrill rushed through him. Why would she lie?

Her blush deepened to a deep rose.

Yves, the groom-to-be, approached him.

Then his fiancée Lainey slid next to him and scooped up his arm.

Jean-Marc realized their energetic conversation attracted the attention of the bride- and groom-to-be.

Tugging at his cufflinks, Yves arched his eyebrows.

Lainey hooked her elbow in his.

Even Alexandre stopped to watch their conversation.

"What's going on here?" Yves straightened his tie and glanced between them. "Livi?"

Livi ducked her head. "I'm sorry, Yves. I didn't mean to cause a scene. Jean-Marc asked my opinion about his pastries."

Yves raised his chin. "And what did you say?"

She stared into Jean-Marc's face. "He clearly has technical skill but lacks creativity in both presentation and preparation."

With a hint of a smile, Alexandre leaned closer. "Indeed? What would you do differently?"

Jean-Marc crumpled his tea towel. This was ridiculous! How dare his father take her side?

"I would change up your *petit fours*. Add something exciting and unexpected." She picked up one and then plopped it on her plate. "These are everyday run-of-the-mill."

He huffed. Sure, he could play along with this game. "What would you change?"

Livi ran a finger over the icing. "You could cut them into heart shapes. Or use fondant instead of icing."

Who was this little critic? Jean-Marc shook his head. He'd heard enough.

"It's true."

Her gaze shot from Yves, to Lainey, and to

Alexandre, then back to him.

"I've watched a few of your shows, and I learned a lot. I don't mean to be rude, but I feel like you are too, too…what's the word?" She snapped her fingers. "You tell the protocol of how it's to be done, but you lack the luster of the art."

Jean-Marc threw out his hands. How could she know of his weakness? He dismissed the thought. Shaking his head, he huffed. What weakness? "And after watching my videos, you think I could learn something from you?"

Swallowing hard, she backed a step. "Is the student better than the master?"

Her cheeks tinged pink again—the color of cotton candy. Warmth swelled in his chest.

She bit her lip. "I don't know anything you don't know. However, you've forgotten the craft is also an art."

She stared right into his soul. A brush of emotion tugged at his heart, but he quickly dismissed it. "Nonsense." He folded his arms across his chest.

A noise at the table drew her gaze.

The little boy dropped a fork. The baby knocked over a glass.

"I have to tend to the kids. Excuse me." She bent her head and disappeared.

Alexandre slapped him on the shoulder. "God has landed a partner in your lap."

"Her?" He jabbed a thumb over his shoulder. A shudder went through him. "No way. I'd rather work with a viper." Shaking his head, Jean-Marc cleared away empty trays. People ate his creations faster than he could fill plates. Was that not proof enough of his genius?

Yves arched a brow. He exchanged looks with his fiancée. "Tell me, Jean-Marc, what are you doing this week?"

He focused solely on clearing empty platters. "Searching for a co-host." He glanced up. "Why?"

Yves tucked an arm around Lainey. "You wouldn't happen to have some spare time, would you? Lainey and I wanted to ask about wedding cakes."

Alexandre already asked him about taking the contract. The wedding, though, was still months away.

"Can you meet with us while you're in town this week?" Yves cocked his head.

"Sure." Jean-Marc frowned. Despite having lots of things to do, he couldn't spite his old friend. He cleared away the *petit fours*. How dare she insult his work! He tasted a small cake. It was a bit soggy in the middle. He left the rest on a plate.

"Do you have time tomorrow?" Lainey prodded him with an elbow.

Jean-Marc raised his head. "Text me when you're free." Swiping the tea towel over his shoulder, he bent to scoop up an empty tray.

Yves nodded and led away Lainey.

"She made a good point." Alexandre brushed the front buttons of his jacket and knitted his fingers together across his chest.

Jean-Marc huffed. "Who? Oh, the nanny? She was rude and ridiculous." He glared at the young lady across the room. What was her name? Livi?

She bent and wiped a nose of a young boy, then made the baby laugh.

Other men would find her maternal caring

endearing or attractive, but he searched for someone with real charisma. He hoped he never would see her again.

Chapter 5

"Look! Fresh snow! We must head to the slopes."
Mr. Gordon sipped his coffee in his bathrobe near the
giant, thirty-foot windows overlooking the valley.
Nearly a foot of fresh powder blanketed everything
from the trees to the ground.

Ugh, of course they wanted to ski on fresh snow.
Shaking her head, Livi wiped spilt milk from where the
kids ate at the table. At eight o'clock in the morning,
Mrs. Gordon was not up yet. "What about our contract?
I'm supposed to have the afternoon off." She planned to
meet Yves and Lainey for lunch. Last night at the party,
she barely got to talk to them.

"We can't miss this opportunity to ski on fresh
snow." He turned and crossed the room to place his
mug on the table. "This experience is what we came to
Switzerland for! I'll add a little more to your bonus for
being so accommodating." With a lightness of step, he
climbed the tread to the loft.

Clearing off the mug, Livi slumped. She would
have the kids for the whole day. *Yippee!* She kicked the
wooden baseboards. Ouch! After a morning of
swimming in the heated pool, she bathed the kids and
dressed them, then took the bus into Vevey.

Jean-Marc was the scarf-man. Well, he was so rude
in the store, even if he did pay for her stuff. And the
party—last night was a disaster. What an egotistical

jerk! Why did she ever watch his awful show? Livi met her idol and mentor and told him straight to his face he was too technical. Yet, he was way more attractive in person. What was she thinking?

With aching shoulders, Livi lifted Alice's stroller onto the bus. Man, she missed having a car. She weaved through the seats and found a spot for her and Henry to sit. She probably ruined the party for Lainey and Yves. She must apologize when they met this afternoon for fondue.

Livi shook her head. What was she doing in this beautiful country? Despite the snow last night, the clouds were gone, and the milky, winter sun greeted them. Snow topped the continuous row of buildings. Strings of lit stars hung across the road. Christmas shouted from every storefront window. Her heart ached. This holiday barely felt like Christmas. She hadn't had a chance to do her normal holiday baking. Creating sweet treats for friends and neighbors was a service she missed. The act gave her more meaning to the busy holiday season. A tiny tear welled in the corner of her eye.

She breathed in. She sacrificed her Christmas break to pay for Wendy's car and to help take care of the Gordons. She squeezed Henry.

At last, the bus arrived.

She descended with some help from an older gentleman. Shielding her eyes from the sun reflecting off the snow, she searched for Yves's figure along the cement balustrade along the water.

Henry clutched her coattails as she crossed the street to the lake.

Yves stood near a flowerbed. He beckoned her.

Eight years passed since she'd seen him last. He was twenty then and had just started his job at Alpine Foods where his father worked. Now, he looked older—more mature. But Yves was born an old man. His dark hair blew in the slight breeze coming off the lake. He wore a dark four-button suit under his wool peacoat. He always wore a suit. In fact, Livi had never seen him not wearing a suit. What little she saw of Lainey, she seemed like a good match. When Livi met her last night, she was fun, confident, and made Yves smile, which he needed.

She pushed the stroller toward him and Lainey. And a third person sat on a bench facing the lake.

The man stood and turned.

Oh, not Jean-Marc. Dread grew in her stomach along with some serious butterflies. Livi glanced away. Gritting her teeth, she hunched her shoulders. Holding up her head, she dared to take a second glance. His dimple was even more adorable in real life. She scowled. But he was rude last night. Some part of her wished Alice would throw up so she could excuse herself and return to the chalet.

Yves gave her air-kisses across her cheeks.

Lainey leaned in for a hug.

Livi hoped she didn't have to greet Jean-Marc with the kisses. She purposefully stayed far away. "Hello!" She faked a smile toward Jean-Marc. "What are you doing here?"

He leaned close for the kisses.

His closeness caught her off guard. Heat rushed to her chest. He smelled of vanilla and musk. She quickly returned the way-too-touchy-feely embrace, her body tingling.

Jean-Marc stuffed his hands into his coat pockets. "Yves and Lainey invited me. We discussed their plans for a wedding cake."

Yves led the way down the promenade lined with a cement balustrade.

Livi pushed Alice's stroller and made a mental note of where Henry was. Though few people strolled along the paved path near the water, she worried he'd lag behind, looking at some interesting trees that sheltered the path on the mountain side. "Oh? And what did you decide on?"

Lainey grinned and gestured with her hands. "Chocolate with chocolate filling with chocolate *ganache* glaze."

Livi brushed hair out of her mouth. "Sounds delicious but rather bland. In my mind, the perfect cake would be more exciting. Maybe you could try complementary flavors like chocolate and orange or raspberry. Even chocolate cassis or mulberries would be interesting. Chocolate-lavender sounds good, or maybe try chocolate and fig!"

"We are kindred spirits!" Lainey clapped her hands. She turned to Jean-Marc. "Perhaps we should rethink just the plain chocolate idea."

Jean-Marc furrowed his brow and crossed his arms. "If you wish, but I promise my chocolate cake is the best in the industry."

Lainey clutched Yves's elbow. "Still, I want a cake that is incomparable. We should explore some other combinations. Don't you think, Yves?"

He nodded in his tight way.

Jean-Marc shot Livi a scowl.

Lainey clapped her hands again. "You two should

work together and create the perfect cake."

Livi nearly choked. Gulping for air, she stopped pushing the stroller. "You want me to work with him?" Dread bubbled up in her chest. His big ego would clog all the room in the kitchen.

"Ha!" Jean-Marc shook his head.

Yves spread his gloved hands. "Why not? You have the technical skills. Livi has the creativity. You'd make the perfect pair."

Jean-Marc thrust up his jaw. "I didn't go to school for years and perfect my business just to work with an amateur." He stalked ahead.

The insult hit her like a smack in the face. She swallowed back a spurt of anger. Snatching at Henry's hand, she jogged to catch up. "You don't think I can keep up in the kitchen?"

Jean-Marc thrust up his jaw. "I know you can't."

Henry raised his little head. His pom-pom on his head bounced. "Miss Livi is the best baker around. Her cookies are the tastiest!"

"Thank you, Henry." Lifting her chin, Livi patted him on the head and secretly smiled at his courageous defense.

Yves stopped short. "I have an idea. Why don't you first ask her to cook a pastry, or you can both cook the same thing, and we can judge which is best? If we like what she's made, you can work together on a cake prototype."

"Either way I lose." Shaking his head, Jean-Marc scowled.

Yves stopped him with a hand on his shoulder. "Either way you win, *mon ami*. You either find yourself someone to work with who has creative ideas, or you get to design the cake yourself. What I fear most is what Livi gets out of the deal." He shot a stare.

Livi blushed and turned away to fuss with Henry's zipper. She'd be a fool not to admit that working with Jean-Marc would be a great opportunity to learn new skills and admire the scenery.

Jean-Marc huffed. "She'd get an opportunity to work with me. If she is up to snuff, then she can refine her skills under the tutelage of one of the greatest pastry chefs in Europe."

"Brilliant." Yves clapped his hand. "What do you say, Livi?"

A chance to work with Jean-Marc? The thought sent shivers through her body. It both thrilled and terrified her. What if she failed? What if she proved herself superior? "Sounds like an interesting challenge." Arching her eyebrow, she faced Jean-Marc. "What would you like me to make?"

"Bring me the perfect *macaron*." He lifted his head and narrowed his eyes. Rubbing his chin scruff, he partially smiled. "In fact, let's make it a competition to see who can make the best *macaron*." He nodded to Yves and Lainey. "They will judge to see whose is best."

Biting her lip, Livi stared out onto the ice-blue lake. Macarons were her albatross—the only cookie that escaped her expertise. She'd have to find a simpler recipe. She wouldn't have time to practice. "But I don't have my equipment or my own kitchen at our rental."

Jean-Marc shrugged. "All right. We'll make them together at my father's apartment here in town. He has the necessary ingredients and equipment."

Her heart thundered. She'd never made a batch of

macarons that turned out right. How would she find the time to perfect them? "When do you want to meet?" She puffed out her chest to show more confidence than she felt.

Jean-Marc lifted an eyebrow. "Tomorrow afternoon."

"I don't have the time off." That space was clearly marked on her calendar.

"Tomorrow night then?"

She nodded.

He held up his phone. "I'll text you the address."

She gave him her phone number. Her heartbeat pulsed in her ears. She swallowed, but her throat was dry. What was she thinking baking in a competition against the world's best pastry chef?

****

Did he seriously promise to work with such an amateur? Jean-Marc paced the galley kitchen in Alexandre's apartment. Jitters rose from his stomach. She would be here any moment.

He checked his appearance in the mirror next to the door. Fine, he was fine. He hadn't asked her to co-host the show. They were just making *macarons* side by side in the kitchen. Rolling out the stress in his neck, he pushed up the sleeves of his dark gray sweater.

The door buzzed. He counted to ten so she wouldn't know he was waiting for her. With a flourish, he turned the knob.

Livi stood on the doorstep.

Her sweet smile spread across her lips. A shot went through him as if he'd been stuck with a hot blade of sugar. How had he never noticed her smile before?

"Welcome." He swept a hand to show her inside.

Thankfully, Alexandre worked tonight. Jean-Marc pointed toward the well-lit food prep area. "You have that half of the kitchen. I will be working over here." Earlier, he set up a hot plate and an older mixer on the dining table and let her use the better appliances in the kitchen. She would need every advantage.

He laid out eggs, almond flour, and both powdered and granulated sugar. How carefully would she weigh each ingredient? Or would she use the dreaded and inaccurate American "cups?" He purposefully didn't leave out the scale. He would see if she asked for it.

With both hands, she swept her hair into a pony. "Thank you for letting me come here to bake."

"Yves and Lainey promised to come in two hours to judge." He nodded toward an apron on the counter.

Rubbing her hands together, she nodded. "Right."

After washing her hands, she wrapped the apron around her small waist. Jean-Marc resisted the urge to help her tie it in the back. Shaking such thoughts from his head, he went to his table to mix and measure, but he watched her like a hawk.

After rolling up her sleeves, she separated the eggs. In the mixer, she beat the whites. "Do you have a scale?" she shouted over the sound.

He raised his eyebrows. "Indeed." From under the counter, he retrieved a small digital scale and laid it nearby. The scent of her perfume enticed him. Nothing attracted him more than smell. He inhaled a hint of cinnamon and orange. Gulping, he moved to the other side of the kitchen near the giant wood table which filled the dining room.

While he simmered together the sugar and the water to form the Italian meringue, he waited for her to do the same.

But instead of doing the same, she weighed and measured the almond flour and the powdered sugar.

If she didn't start the sugar mixture soon, her egg whites would be over-beaten, and the delicate cookies would be too dry. He bit his lip. He vowed not to say anything. This was a competition. She had to prove herself worthy.

She turned off the mixer.

Too soon. He glanced over. What was she doing? To make these properly, she would need to pour the hot sugar and water into the mixer at precisely 123C degrees. She shouldn't be stopping the mixer.

She scooped out the egg whites into her almond and sugar mixture.

He slapped his hand across his face. She failed. She couldn't even make *macarons*. He would win for sure!

Holding the bowl with one hand, she mixed with the other.

He poured the boiling sugar and water mixture into his egg whites and shouted over the sound of the mixer. "*Macaronage* is the method for perfectly mixing your *macarons*. You don't want to over-mix or you will lose all the stiffening of the egg white, and your *macarons* will be too flat."

She turned and grinned. "That's why I sing my song. If I sing it, that's usually enough time to mix it."

"You sing?" Shaking his head, he leaned closer. Who ever heard of a singing cook?

"I sang in choir in high school. I even took State in Solo and Ensemble."

Her smile was infectious. He couldn't help himself. "What will you sing?"

With a hint of a smile, she lifted her chin. "Well, today, I'll sing a Christmas song. 'Angels We Have Heard On High.' " She softly sang the first verse. When she got to the chorus, she belted out the "gloria" and mixed the egg whites with the powdered sugar and almond mixture.

Jean-Marc bit back a smile and stared into the white, snowy peaks in his mixer. This woman was nuts! A hint of warmth sneaked into his heart as he mixed his Italian meringue.

"Come on. Join me!" She waved a hand.

Her invitation melted him. On the third verse, he joined her in French, adding his baritone to her sweet melody. A lightness filled his chest. He immediately shook it away.

"Oh, that's funny." She stuck her spoon and tested the consistency. "The song is slightly different in French."

Nodding, he sifted the almond and powdered sugar into the egg whites. "The French version contains more syllables, so the tune is a little different. The carol is French, you know. Someone translated it into English." When a drop of mixture flipped out onto his hand, he licked his knuckle.

"Is it?" She lifted the spoon and let the mixture drip into the bowl. "The consistency is perfect. It worked."

"I'll have to remember your trick of singing." Could he add songs to his show? What would his audience think?

"Do you have a piping bag?" She squinted. "A pastry bag?"

"Of course." Why hadn't he retrieved them earlier?

Dropping his bowl, he stalked over and opened the cabinet over her head. Her soft curls were as sculpted caramel—dark and silky. He resisted the urge to run his fingers through them. He laid a cloth pastry bag on the counter near her.

Using a big spoon, she scooped mixture into the bag. "Oh, a reusable one. I hope you're doing the dishes." She winked.

He leaned against the counter near her. She was not nearly as repulsive as he originally thought. She was actually kind of…fun…in the kitchen. "Normally, I hire someone to do the unpleasant task, but I will do the dirty deed today." He grabbed another for himself and went back to his table and piped. He checked on his *protégé*. Her piping techniques weren't terrible. She held the bag properly and kept it at the right angle. "Who taught you?"

She glanced up. "You did. I watched your shows."

He grinned. "I'm an excellent teacher." He hoped she found his compliment funny. "At first, you didn't admit to watching my shows." A tinge of color reached her cheeks. She bent over perfect circles. Her lack of answer thrilled him. And she was a good learner, as evidenced by her technique. Except she still had some flaws.

She continued piping small blobs of mixture on the mats.

Leaving his own to cure, he entered the kitchen. "May I offer a critique?"

"Uh, sure." She lifted her pastry bag and held it.

"You're a little off on your technique. Let me show you." He grasped her hand still around the bag and lifted both her hand and the bag. A zing of lightning went through him as he touched her hand. With a beating heart, he backed away. "There. Straight up. You will have a more consistent shape." Although she still made them with the wrong ingredients. He'd be surprised if they turned out at all.

"Thank you." She smiled.

Her smile sent his heart careening to his ribs, as if he'd eaten the most divine fondant-covered *éclair*. Gulping, he returned to his table.

When finished, she washed her hands in the sink and ran the bag under the water. "Just so you won't have so much to do later. This stuff is a real bear to clean once it dries."

"Thank you." Keeping his head to clean off the table, he hoped she didn't see his growing attraction.

After forty-five minutes, the rounds developed a skin.

Once the circles were tacky, he slid them in the oven. "Ladies first." He watched as hers grew spectacular feet—the edges around the cookies had a nice height when they rose in the oven. He couldn't believe his eyes. How did that happen? She must've cheated somehow. "The real test is the taste."

The doorbell buzzed.

He slapped his hands together. "Our friends are here." Crossing the flat, he opened the door. Lainey wore the ugliest Christmas sweater and jeans. Yves still wore his usual suit and tie. "The *macarons* are just coming out of the oven." He showed them the couch. "We'll let them cool before we serve them." He rejoined Livi in the kitchen. "All right, now for the buttercream filling."

"What flavor are you creating?"

He held up a finger. "I'll let you choose first. So, what are you making?" Whatever she wanted, he hoped he had on hand. "My kitchen is open to you. Feel free to browse." He opened a cupboard filled with items. He set a box of small vials filled with oil essences of all flavors.

She studied the vials—pistachio, green tea, rose water, lavender, fruits of all kinds, and many natural flavorings. "I want to try a Christmas flavor. When I was a young child, my father left a chocolate orange in the toe of our stocking instead of a real orange. The gesture always made me smile. If you have orange flavoring, I'll do orange and chocolate."

He plucked through small vials of essences. "Sounds delicious."

"It's one of the few memories I have of him."

"Oh?" He didn't want to pry, but he cared. He found the orange flavoring.

She twisted the tea towel in her hands. Her eyes focused downward. "He left me, my mom, and my sister Wendy when we were young. I was ten, and my sister was eight."

"I'm sorry to hear that." He set the small vial in front of her. He resisted the urge to touch her hand again. "Go on. Why did he leave?" He couldn't imagine growing up without a father. Alexandre was everything to him—mentor as well as father.

Sighing, she shrugged. "Maybe he was overwhelmed by raising kids, or maybe he found a better life somewhere else. Either way, my mom worked hard to support us."

Jean-Marc hadn't seen his mom in a long time. "I understand. My parents divorced when I was fourteen.

Mum is Swiss. She didn't want my father to be a chef. Perhaps she thought my father's working in a kitchen was lowly or beneath her." Jean-Marc shrugged. "Cooking is his passion. She didn't understand it." His confession surprised him. He rarely shared his personal history with other people. Instead, he preferred the illusion that his life was perfect. He coughed. "So, orange-chocolate?"

Shrugging, she raised her brows. "Or other winter or Christmassy flavors. Peppermint, pumpkin—"

"Pumpkin?" A bit of repulsion raked through him. "For sweets?"

Livi threw back her head and laughed. "Americans love pumpkin spice. They put it in their coffee, cereal—everywhere."

Jean-Marc grabbed his stomach and stuck out his tongue as if gagging. "Yuck!"

Livi slapped him on the shoulder. "Oh, stop. Americans are weird."

"Yes, you are. Pumpkin coffee?" He mused. "Do you really?"

"Sadly, yes. The flavoring a seasonal thing. And it's more like the spices we put in pumpkin pie—allspice, cinnamon, and nutmeg."

Hmm, that was better, but still! He shook his head. "What other flavors?"

She glanced up to the ceiling, counting on her fingers. "I considered eggnog, buttered rum, pomegranate…"

She was passionate about her flavorings. A light buzzed in his brain. Her creativity amused him. "I don't have eggnog or pomegranate."

"All right…" She picked through the oils in little

vials. "I'll do...peppermint." She picked up the vial. "Can I use those, too?" She pointed toward the small tree his father put up and decorated only with candy canes.

He nodded. "I said you can use any ingredient we have." He snatched up the orange essence. "And I will do your orange chocolate." And since Lainey loved chocolate, it was his ace in the hole. Had Livi forgotten? He smirked as he heated cream for a chocolate *ganache* and cut up sixty percent dark chocolate. After pouring the heated cream over the chocolate, he mixed in orange flavoring.

She gathered candy canes, crushed them in the mortar and pestle, and mixed it into the peppermint buttercream.

"Let me try a taste." He stuck in his pinky and licked it. A burst of Christmas memories spread through him on the breath of peppermint. "Hm, not bad. But these are still not real *macarons*."

"What?" She piped the buttercream onto the shells. "What do you mean?"

He stuck his hands on his hips. "You cheated."

She lowered her brow. "I didn't cheat."

"You didn't use Italian meringue." He wagged a finger. He wasn't sure if he was joking or serious. A mixture of curiosity and respect tingled within him. She batted her a hand in the air at him. "That's way too much work, and if I do them that way, mine always fail. So I created this version, which is close enough. I bet you can't tell the difference." She licked a blob of buttercream from her thumb.

Offended, he huffed. "It's not whether I can tell a difference, although I can, even with my eyes closed.

You must pass the test with the bride- and groom-to-be."

"Well, close your eyes and open up. The first one is ready." She sandwiched the peppermint buttercream between two layers of crisp *macaron* shell.

He closed his eyes and opened his mouth. The *macaron* melted on his tongue. Scents of peppermint energized his senses. The cookie refreshed him. Memories of Christmas mornings filled his mind. He opened his eyes. A smile broke on his lips.

Livi stared with her brows raised. "What did you think?"

"Not bad." He grinned. "You still cheated." Jean-Marc arranged a half-dozen of his chocolate orange on the plate, then stacked hers alongside them. He took the plate into the living room and laid them on the coffee table before Yves and Lainey.

"Honest judgment: which *macarons* are better?" He spread his hands wide. He shot a glance to Livi. She tried hard, but she was not up to snuff.

Yves slid a peppermint in his mouth. "Perfection!"

Lainey followed suit. "These are fantastic! Chewy yet crunchy. I love them! Whoever made these is a master."

Moving the towel behind her back, Livi beamed.

Jean-Marc scowled. "Try the other."

Yves bit into one. An eyebrow rose. "Very good, but a little heavy." He focused on the plate in front of him.

Lainey shoved the whole thing in her mouth.

Jean-Marc twisted his tea towel.

Lainey nodded. "Not bad, but not as good as the peppermint. Sorry."

"I win!" Livi jumped up. She waved her tea towel in the air. "They liked them! They really liked them!"

Jean-Marc crossed his arms. "But you didn't make them how they are supposed to be made."

She punched the air. "But this method is much more approachable. Everyday people can try a simple recipe. Maybe on your new show, you could, every once in a while, make things that everyday people can make. And, as you see, they were good!"

Jean-Marc scowled. Her opinions about his show rubbed him the wrong way. What did she know about television or the business or pastry-making, for that matter?

Yves stood and buttoned his suit. "I'm afraid we have to go. However, I'm glad you'll be planning the prototype of the cake together. Let us know when you have it ready."

Jean-Marc enjoyed his time with her in the kitchen, but could he work with her to bake a prototype of the cake? He wasn't so sure about that. He had a terrible track record with partners.

Chapter 6

At last, an afternoon off, all to herself. The Gordons dropped Livi off in Vevey before they had their family time in town. She told them she planned to do some shopping. Instead, she climbed the stairs to Jean-Marc's apartment. With trembling hands, she pushed the buzzer. Just because she won the friendly *macaron* competition didn't mean Jean-Marc wanted to work with her on this project. She smiled. His expression when she won was priceless. He dropped his jaw and crossed his arms. She might like his displeased/horrorified expression better than his dimpled smile.

The door swung open with a whoosh of air. Jean-Marc stood in the hall. He had on a chef coat—not as tailored at the one he used on screen, but still attractive.

He arched a brow. "What are you smiling about?"

She'd rather die than tell him how hot he looked. "Just savoring my win yesterday."

He huffed and waved her inside. "Just because you can make a decent, albeit *incorrect, macaron* doesn't mean you are a certified pastry chef with years of experience."

She nodded. "Indeed. I have lots to learn."

Inside, the apartment still smelled of peppermint. She wasn't sure if it was from the buttercream or from the candy canes hanging from the small, live tree. The whole apartment smelled of Christmas. Fragrant oranges with whole cloves puncturing the skins in decorative designs hung from boughs. The decorations were sparse compared to Mrs. Gordon's house. A few greeting cards hung on a wall. Someone painted fake snow in the corners of the windows.

He pulled back a chair at the sturdy wooden table. "Here. Sit."

With nerves racing through her, she slid into the chair. On the table were different types of baking chocolate, the cassis, mulberries, and figs. Already ideas of combinations sprang into her head.

He paced behind the table. "Now instead of competing, we work together."

"Do you think you can handle it?" She loved to poke with her words.

He lowered his eyebrows. "What do you mean?"

She cracked a partial smile. "You don't have a track record of playing nicely with others."

He lifted his chin. "And you are exasperating."

But he didn't sound annoyed. "Indeed." She leaned forward in the chair with her elbows on the table inspecting the ingredients. "What have you gathered?"

"Though you suggested using original ideas combined with the chocolate, adding fruit can alter the acidity of the cake, the texture, and even the crumb. So if you want something that will please our potential clients—"

"Our potential clients?" A tingle of energy fluttered in her stomach.

"If we create a recipe that makes Lainey and Yves happy, I will pay you five percent of the fee."

"Five percent? That seems a little low for the

creative engineer." She bit her lips to keep from grinning.

"Fine." He crossed his arms across his chest. "Ten percent. Remember, I still have to do all the baking and the decorating on the day of the event."

"Sounds good." Getting paid ten percent for doing something she loved made her heart sing. Making cakes was what she was born to do! "All right. Let's get started!" She clapped her hands together.

He pulled out a pad of paper and ran through the combinations she'd already listed. "All we have to do is make a prototype of each one and hope they don't come out too wet or too dry."

She stood and inclined her head. "Let's get to the kitchen then."

Lowering his brow, Jean-Marc slid the pencil between his teeth, leaving his hands free to move the ingredients to the kitchen.

Livi grinned at the adorable tic.

He held out an apron.

She slipped it over her head and struggled to find the ties.

Removing the pencil for a second, he lifted his chin. "Let me help you." He snatched at the ends.

She felt a tug at her waist, and his touch brushed against her back. His closeness sent shivers down her spine. She gulped. In the kitchen, she peeled, sliced, and boiled fruit. Using a food mill, she twisted the handle over the holes to deseed most of the fruit, leaving just the essence.

After sifting dry ingredients, melting the chocolate in the double-boiler, and measuring the milk, Jean-Marc prepared six, four-inch cake pans to bake their recipes.

She danced a delicate dance around him, working in harmony. "Where's the sugar?"

With his pencil still in his mouth, he pointed toward a cupboard.

"Is the pencil like a bit to keep you from saying something you regret?" She found the bin and lugged the sugar over to the counter next to a pad of paper.

With a click of his teeth, he removed the pencil. "Very funny. The pencil helps me concentrate. And then I always know where it is when I need to make notations. I always do this when I create a new recipe."

"When was the last time you created a new recipe?"

Throwing the pencil to the counter, Jean-Marc froze. "A long time ago." Finally, he placed both hands on the counter and lowered his head.

A story lurked beneath the surface, but she wouldn't get it out of him now. "As a novice, I'm not afraid to make mistakes."

His head snapped up, and he removed the chocolate from the burner. "As a professional, I know the rules, and I know how to break them in ways that create fantastic results." He grabbed her fruit compotes and mixed them with the chocolate and flour. "Taste." Nabbing a spoon, he dipped it into the batter.

With more tenderness than she expected, he held the spoon out for her to taste. She opened her mouth.

He slipped in the spoon.

Chocolate and figs mellowed over her tongue. The sweet fig tempered the bitter aftertaste of the chocolate. She raised her eyebrows. "The batter's quite good, actually."

"I'll try." He dug the spoon in again and tasted the batter. A slow smile crept across his face. "We'll wait and see how its crumb turns out. That's the real test."

Out of the six cakes, three included the fruit compotes in the mix. The other three were plain chocolate with the compotes to be used as filling. At last, the six were in the oven. Livi's feet ached. Her neck hurt.

Jean-Marc slapped his tea towel over his shoulder and leaned against the counter.

Her heart stuttered. Why was he staring like that?

****

Jean-Marc stared at Livi. Half of her caramel-colored hair tumbled from its ponytail in the back of her head. Her cheeks glowed pink after the exhausting few hours. He couldn't remember when he'd enjoyed baking more.

Livi lowered her gaze to the dishes. "I should work on these. I know chefs never do their own dishes."

"I'll help."

Elbow to elbow and shoulder to shoulder, Jean-Marc washed dishes. Her hair curled in ringlets at her neck. He resisted the urge to bend and kiss the smooth skin there or clasp one of those strands and let the silky threads run through his fingers. The scent of her rattled him. What was he thinking? In a few days, he would return to London, and she would go home to America. They had no future together. He needed to focus on finding a partner.

Could his father be right? Could she really be an equal in the kitchen? Her skills were unpracticed—untested even. But she had the desire, the drive, and the patience—all important qualities for a master pastry chef.

But then, being in the kitchen with her was so natural and so pleasing. He could see her on set with him, asking questions so he could explain the technique to his audience. Her naïveté would complement his prowess in the kitchen. A slight smile pushed its way to his lips.

"What are you thinking?"

He raised his head. Too bad he'd been focusing too much on the dishes and not enough on what happened in the room.

She'd dried all the dishes and stacked them.

He scrambled to come up with a plausible explanation. No way could he ever let her know he was thinking about the two of them. "Oh, I was just thinking of Christmas. What holiday traditions do you have? What would you be doing if you were at home?"

Livi sighed with an exaggerated frown. "In Boston, I'd be baking cookies—lots of different varieties—to give to my neighbors."

"You are from Boston?"

She shook her head and put away dishes. "I moved from Indiana to Boston so I could nanny the Gordons' kids. You'd be surprised how few people in small-town Indiana have nannies. Boston was the best choice. I've been with them for three years now. I remember the day they brought Alice home from the hospital. They asked me to do her nightly feedings so Mrs. Gordon could work in the morning."

He handed her a clean dish. "They seemed to be demanding bosses."

Taking the dish, she shrugged. "It's a job."

"I see. What would you do if you were home?"

"Oh, that was loads of fun." Her eyes lit up. She leaned against the counter. "My sister and I caroled with friends, went on sleigh rides in the country, and attended parties. So many parties."

"You don't go to parties now?" He finished the last dish, rinsed it, and placed it on the drying rack.

Shaking her head, she picked up the dish and dried it. "No. Mostly I stay home and watch the kids so the Gordons can go to parties." She smiled a half smile.

"Well, I hope while you are here, you will have a great Christmas. Switzerland has many fun holiday activities."

She shrugged. "I guess so. It's just not as fun to wander around by myself. I prefer being with the kids to being alone."

The buzzer sounded. He opened the oven. The smell of chocolate cake, punctuated with a hint of fruity tanginess, punched him in the face. He pulled out the pans and tested the center. "Perfect!" He laid them on the counter to cool.

"I'll start the filling." Livi grabbed more ingredients, mixing the fruit compote with sugar.

After thirty more minutes, he filled the cooled cakes. "Now for *ganache* frosting." He poured the thick, decadent chocolate and cream mixture over the cakes, the syrupy glaze dripping through the mesh.

Leaning close, Livi stuck a finger under the cakes.

"No tasting." He still held the bowl with both hands or he would've rapped her knuckles with a wooden spoon, like his instructors had whenever a student dared to sneak a taste. Then he felt fingers running up and down his ribs. With a guffaw, he nearly dropped the bowl. "Ah-ah! No tasting! Tickling is not very nice."

With quick action, she dipped a finger into the chocolate. Grinning, she licked her finger free of chocolate. Then, she swooped her wiggling fingers into his ribs again.

He clamped his elbows to his chest. His ribs were so ticklish. The drizzle went off the cakes. "See what you made me do?" A burble of laughter erupted from his throat.

With a huge grin, she swiped at the trickle of chocolate on the counter. "Yum!" She giggled.

"You naughty girl. Someone needs to teach you a lesson." He held the bowl above her. Most of the chocolate was gone now. Only a few drips left the bowl.

She tipped back her head and caught the chocolate drips with her tongue. "See? You can't outsmart me!"

A zing went through him. "Ha! A challenge?" He swiped a bit of residue from the bowl and wiped it across her cheek. Laughter burst from his throat. "There! No more snitching."

She doubled over, laughing and grabbing for a rag to wipe her face.

The doorbell rang. Jean-Marc, still shaking from laughter, crossed the room and turned the knob.

Yves and Lainey stood on the doorstep.

He tried to control his snickers, but to no avail. "We just finished the prototypes!"

Yves's gaze dropped to his messy chef's uniform. "Having fun, I see."

Jean-Marc lowered his head to inspect himself. Smears of chocolate marred his white coat. He raised his eyebrows, laughed, and waved them in. "We finished!"

Lainey clapped her hands. "Your apartment smells delicious."

After plating the six cakes, Livi untied her apron and sat at the table, ready for the taste test.

Handing each of them a fork, Jean-Marc stifled a laugh and cut the first cake.

Yves took a bite. "Mmm. Very good. It's moist but still maintains an excellent crumb." He saluted with his fork.

After her bite, Lainey nodded, her eyes lighting up.

They tried all six cakes.

Lainey landed her hands in her lap. "I can't tell which is the best. They are all so good, and all exceeded my expectations. You two have outdone yourselves. Thank you. I would be happy to serve any of these cakes at our wedding."

"Thank you." Jean-Marc breathed a sigh of relief.

Lainey touched Yves's shoulder. "We'll go home and decide. Thank you!" She scooted back her chair and rose. Gathering her coat, she hugged Livi. "You two are brilliant in the kitchen."

After seeing them out, Jean-Marc closed the door. He still wasn't convinced Livi was the one. Was she ready for this crazy lifestyle? Should he keep searching for a partner?

Chapter 7

Whitecaps formed on Lake Geneva. In the punishing wind, Livi pushed the stroller around the balustrade lining the promenade. Clouds hung low over the snow-capped mountains. Her fingers felt like chunks of ice. If only she'd remembered to bring her gloves.

The whole gray day loomed before her. The Gordons asked her to take the kids all day—again—on one of her days off. Mrs. Gordon also insisted the kids get out of the chalet to see the sights and get exercise.

Livi gritted her teeth against the wind. Bonus, she reminded herself. She was doing this for the bonus to pay off Wendy's credit card. Desperate to turn around the day, she searched for anything to be happy about. Two lovely, white birds floated nearby. "Look, Henry. See the swans?"

Henry pointed to the lake. "What's that in the water?"

Livi stared past the swans. How bizarre! A giant fork stuck tine-side down in the water. "I have no idea. Let's go down there, shall we?" She sped up her pace.

Henry nodded and clung to the stroller. "Where did everyone go?"

"I don't know." Livi looked around. No one strolled near the lake. She peeked up the streets. Not a single soul crossed the streets. It seemed the entire town of Vevey closed from noon to two. Townspeople weren't even out on the streets, kind of like a weird Twilight Zone where everyone disappeared for two hours.

At last, they reached the fork. Livi stared and shrugged. *Why?*

"I'm tired." Henry dropped his chin to his chest.

Earlier, she bought three pastries at a small shop. She sighed. "Here we can sit on the bench and eat our yummies. But don't tell your mom we ate so much sugar today, okay?"

He raised his head, staring at the fork. "I'm cold."

His little chin shuddered above his reddened nose. "Here, snuggle with me under Alice's blankets." She lifted the toddler out of the stroller and sat her on her lap. She spread the blankets over the three of them. Warmth from all their bodies collected under the fuzzy blanket. Today would be a long day. Maybe after the kids went to bed and, if the Gordons weren't home yet, she could sneak into the sauna. Being warm sounded so good right now.

Alice and Henry munched on a *pain au chocolat*.

Despite the wind, the clouds hung low and heavy. Water lapped along the black rocks. Although sometimes the lake shone like a glacier blue gem, today the lake was a dull gray.

Baking the cakes a few days ago thrilled her. But Jean-Marc was so full of himself and had a large ego. The dimple? She never saw it. Did she imagine admiration shining in his eyes when she baked? Livi shook her head. No use harboring those feelings. Men like Jean-Marc weren't looking for girls like her. They searched for perfection.

Licking her lips, she lifted her favorite pastry—a *religieuse*—or nun, from its envelope. A small *choux* pastry sat on top of a larger one. The *pâtissier* piped chocolate buttercream around the two to attach them and to form the "nun's" collar. A bit of chocolate fondant on the side formed a sort of cape. She bit off the nun's "head." Creamy and decadent chocolate filling reached her taste buds. "Hey, guess what we get to do today."

"What?" Henry squinted. Little, flaky crumbs clung to his lip.

Livi brushed them away. "Your mom asked me to decorate our chalet for Christmas."

Henry's eyes lit up. "Can we get a Christmas tree?"

"Of course." She had no idea where to get a tree.

"And make gingerbread?"

"Maybe." She didn't know if she could buy the ingredients, and her memorized recipe called for American measurements.

For the first time that morning, Henry smiled and flashed a thumbs-up, kicking his feet back and forth. "Can I play by the lake?"

Biting and chewing again, she nodded. "Just don't get too close to the water."

Henry flashed another thumbs-up.

Sliding from Livi's lap to toddle on the walking path, Alice held her pastry and sogged it to death between her gums and little pearly teeth.

Finished with her pastry, Livi should probably go find a park somewhere, but the scenery was so beautiful and relaxing by the lake. Slouching, she shoved her hands into her pockets. The mountains reached the clouds. The huge and awe-inspiring mountains encircled the lake.

"Oh, hello."

Livi craned her neck to see who addressed her.

Wearing a dark jacket, Jean-Marc slid on the bench.

He hadn't shaved since she last saw him. A few days' growth stubbled his chin. Livi's heart leaped to her ribcage. She sat up. Her chest constricted. "What are you doing here?" She scooped Alice onto her lap. He flashed his endearing dimple at her. She must not fall for his charm.

"I was at the *musée d'alimentation*." He jabbed a finger behind him. "The Food Museum."

She careened her neck to the warehouse-sized building near the edge of the lake. "Is that why a fork is in the lake?"

Grinning, he leaned back and kicked out his feet and crossed them at the ankles. "No, a giant was eating here right where you sit and dropped his utensil into the lake."

Shaking her head, she returned his grin. "All right. I deserved that one."

Henry slipped on a rock, letting out a small yelp. His hand landed in dark pebbles.

She bolted forward, nearly dropping Alice. "You okay?" she called.

"I'm fine." Regaining his balance, he brushed his hands on his jacket.

An idea lit upon Livi's mind. She turned and faced Jean-Marc. "Do you know where to find a Christmas tree?"

He lifted his brows. "Actually, I do."

Henry dropped a rock and came running. "Oh, boy!

Are you going to help us?" He stood in front of Jean-Marc.

Standing so he wouldn't see her warm face, she slid Alice into her stroller. "He doesn't have time for that."

"Actually, my afternoon is free."

Heart beating, Livi swiped her hair out of her face and turned to face him. Would he really want to come along? "The tree can't be too big. We have to take the bus back up to Moleson."

He stuck out his lips. "I can drive you home. I have my father's car."

"I couldn't ask you to do that." Swallowing hard, she shook her head. She had already spent way too much time with him. If she spent any more, she might be persuaded to actually like the egotistical jerk.

He lowered his chin and stared. "You're not asking. I'm volunteering. You need to let people help you."

"I let people help me." She huffed.

"Do you?"

He leaned close enough for Livi to see every dark shaft of stubble on his chin and every lash of his eyes. He smelled heavenly—of vanilla and musk.

An older woman in high heels and a fur coat stalked by with a small-breed dog. Her gaze wandered to Alice and then to Henry.

"*Quelle belle famille.*" She smiled and nodded.

Jean-Marc hid a smile behind his hand.

"What did she say?" Livi asked when the lady passed.

He rolled his eyes upward. "She said we're a beautiful family."

A zing went through Livi. A flash of heat warmed her. "Oh, my! We should probably get out of here. I'm so sorry."

"Don't be."

What an assumption! Did people actually think they were together? She guessed they looked like a family. She gulped. How embarrassing!

"I know the perfect place to buy a Christmas tree."

Thankfully, Jean-Marc changed the subject. "Where?" Her hands trembled.

He stood and nodded toward the west end of the lake. "At the Christmas market, of course. It's only a ten-minute train ride to Montreux. Then we don't have to find parking or walk."

Bending, she cupped her hands around Henry's face. "Want to go to a Christmas market?"

Henry tilted his head. "What's a Christmas market?"

"A place where you can see Christmas come to life." Jean-Marc winked.

He was charming with children, just not with women.

"Can we go?" Henry tugged on Livi's coat.

She buckled a squirming Alice in her seat. "Um, sure." She brushed a windblown strand of hair out of her face with shaking fingers. Why was she so nervous?

He took her hand in his bare fingers.

The warmth of his touch flooded her. Electricity from the connection zinged in her heart.

"Follow me." Dropping her hand, he grabbed the stroller and pushed Alice across the street. At a bus stop, he lifted Alice's stroller onto the bus.

"Um, thank you." Holding Henry's hand, Livi

climbed up the big steps.

People filled every seat. So, this was where all the townspeople were.

In the back, a man with a nose as big and as red as a strawberry sang Christmas carols off-tune. She caught a whiff of spices and the tangy scent of alcohol. Who drank hot mulled wine from paper cups in the afternoon?

"Can we get a drink?" Henry's large brown eyes lit up.

"No, honey. That's for adults only."

He crossed his arms across his chest.

The strawberry-nosed man opened his mouth and belted a garbled version of "Hark! the Herald Angels Sing." A Santa hat clung to his graying head. He swayed—not only from the moving bus. He tried to get other people to join in. Most just stared.

At Montreux, Jean-Marc lowered Alice down the stairs.

Crowds of people lined the streets, huddled deep within their jackets.

Along the north side of the Grand Rue, about a hundred miniature versions of the Gordons' wooden chalet lined the street. Each steep, peaked roof was decorated and painted in the Swiss traditional style, with ornate wood cutouts and bright colors. Lights lined each sloped roof. Music played somewhere distant.

Henry widened his eyes. A huge grin lit up his face.

"Come!" Jean-Marc gestured with his head.

Crowds pressed against her shoulders as she walked hand in hand with Henry on the sidewalk underneath the store verandas and the chalets. Each little steep, pitched-roof house showed their wares—wooden kitchen tools, candy, ornaments. She bought two ornaments and a handful of fresh-cut spruce boughs for the table.

Scents of butter, sugar, and flour cooking swirled at a Belgian waffle stand. Children laughed at the rainbow of colors at the gummy candy stand. Soft scarfs, fuzzy handmade mittens, polished wooden toys, delicate glass ornaments, handcrafted soaps, glowing honey, colorful jellies, spicy licorice, scented wreaths, and wooden *crèches* were all crafted by local artisans. She bought a winter hat for her sister made from local wool, and two wooden toys for Henry and Alice while they stared at the candy. While Jean-Marc stood in a line for bratwursts, she sneaked over to another chalet and bought him a wooden spoon. She crossed the street to the tables under the lakeside pavilion. Nearby, vendors cooked fried rice, kabobs, and chestnuts over open fires. Children decorated Christmas cookies at a table.

The scent of cinnamon and spice of the darkened cookies reached her nose. They weren't quite gingerbread. She smelled a hint of citrus. "What are these?"

Jean-Marc grinned. "They're *lebkuchen*. A German cookie. I'll have to show you how to make them sometime." He found a spot at an empty table.

With a buzz in her stomach, she helped Alice eat some bun and fed Henry his bratwurst in small bites.

When they finished, Jean-Marc rose from his seat. "Come! I have more to show you." He passed more craft tables, littered with scraps of paper and glue bottles, glitter, and pipe cleaners.

Alice fussed, wiping her hand across her face.

Henry tugged at her sleeve. "When are we going to get the tree?" His little legs lagged.

Livi wasn't sure the kids could handle much more of the stimulating Christmas circus. "We're almost done."

Jean-Marc headed away from the crowd to a tall, stone cathedral. Someone built a temporary, split-rail fence around the front of the church. Inside, live sheep, two cows, and a donkey rested on straw. A little stable, fashioned from wood, was softly lit in the back of the make-shift pen. Life-sized figures of the Holy Family waited for the manger to be filled.

A quiet reverence settled on her. The moment felt real and intense.

Away from the music, the crowds, the lights, she leaned Henry against the fence to pet the donkey. She petted his velvet nose. The sharp scent of hay clung in the air.

Jean-Marc leaned close and petted the animal, too. His gaze rested upon Livi.

A closeness surrounded the quiet scene. Twilight colored the sky in darkened shades. The sun set early around those mountains. A fresh breeze blew through her. She held her breath. She didn't want to break the spell—the magic binding this place.

But Henry tugged on her sleeve again.

She laid a hand on Jean-Marc's forearm. "Shall we get a tree and go home? The kids will need a break from such an exciting day." Hopefully, the Gordons finished shopping. Night fell and a cooler breeze swept up from the lake.

He placed his hand on hers and nodded.

The tenderness of his gesture thrilled her. When he lifted his gentle touch, an icy breeze met her hand. How she yearned for his warmth.

Across the square, a man in a goofy coat and an apron sold trees.

Jean-Marc picked out one—not too big, not too tall. He slid a fistful of cash into the vendor's hand.

"I have money." Livi snatched at his arm.

Jean-Marc shook his head. "I know. But I do too. And I want to pay."

Warmth filled her as they left the square. This time, she pushed Alice.

Henry gripped the side of the package-laden stroller.

Jean-Marc lugged the tree.

When she stepped up into the warmth of the bus, she noticed everyone stared at the tree.

Jean-Marc grinned and stood with the tree in an area without seats.

She sat in a seat with Henry curled under her arm. Livi caught Jean-Marc's gaze over Henry's head.

He smiled.

Her whole soul burst into flame. She returned his smile. Maybe he wasn't as awful as she originally thought. Or maybe he was just playing her?

****

Back as Jean-Marc's father's apartment, he found the car in the parking garage for residents underneath the building. His hand ached from carrying the tree, but he didn't want to let on how heavy it was. He opened the car doors with a key fob.

Henry crawled in the backseat.

"Will you be able to strap her in?" He arched his

brow at Alice. Babies needed special seating when he offered her a ride. He didn't want to risk the toddler's life.

"Her stroller is her car seat."

"Ah!" He leaned the tree against the car, then went back inside to retrieve a rolling pin, his scale, and more equipment for baking. Earlier, Livi mentioned the kids wanted to make cookies, so he picked up the hard-to-find ingredients, too. With shaking hands, he placed the items in a bag. What was he doing? He was lending his father's tool to a woman he barely knew. But Livi was different from any woman he'd ever worked with. She filled him with a greater desire to create.

At last, he found a roll of twine. When he returned, he tied the tree onto the rooftop of the small car. He shook his head. He felt a little like a family. Livi strapped in Henry into a seatbelt while he tied a tree to his car. He felt strangely whole and complete. He shook the feeling from him. Opening the door, he slid inside, the warmth calming his nerves.

Livi leaned closer. "I've got directions on my phone. The roads get a little snowier up there."

He nodded and started the car. For the first bit of the trip, he fought traffic in town. Halfway up the mountain, the snow piled up on the side of the roads, but the roads themselves were clear.

"Here." She pointed.

A large chalet was built into the side of the mountain. He lugged the tree to the door and waited.

She unlocked it. "The Gordons aren't back yet."

Inside, the tree shrank. The ceilings rose at least two stories, maybe three. "Where would you like this?"

"The tree looks small in here with thirty-foot

ceilings." She shrugged and glanced around. "Near the fireplace, I guess. Henry, help me unload these bags. Alice fell asleep in the car. Let me put her in her bed."

While she attended to Alice, he admired the view. Even in the darkness, the mountains were impressive. He always missed the mountains when in London. Switzerland was home, his beautiful country. His father's family made a lot of sacrifices to come here from Poland.

Livi thundered up the giant, wooden spiral staircase. "I put her in her parents' room."

Some part of him didn't want to leave. Yet, he didn't want things to get awkward. He removed his keys from his pocket.

"Would you like to stay and help us make cookies?"

Heat flashed in his chest. "I would love to." He replaced his keys and removed his jacket. In fact, he was hoping she would ask. She was right when she said the kitchen was ill-equipped for baking. It was small, but all kitchens were small in Switzerland. It just lacked all his equipment. Thankfully, he brought stuff to make biscuits.

"We'll just have to make do. I couldn't find cookie cutters, but I figured we could just cut out whatever shapes with a knife."

"I am very good at that." He rolled up his sleeves. He weighed the dry ingredients and spices she bought from the store.

Henry stirred the wet ingredients. He poured all the molasses into the bowl and measured with the water.

"These cookies might turn out a little strange because it's not exactly the same. I noticed your cinnamon comes from a different place and has a distinct taste." She snitched a finger of dough from the bowl. "Yum, not bad. Not quite right, but not bad."

He stole a taste. Molasses wasn't his favorite, but her recipe wasn't horrible. "Now what?"

She read her phone. "Now we refrigerate for two hours." She wrapped the dough and stuck the lump in the fridge.

"What should we do now?" Henry washed his hands free of molasses.

"Now, we decorate the tree."

"Yahoo!" Henry climbed down from the counter and grabbed a bag of chocolate ornaments.

"Let's set up the tree first." She found a pair of scissors in a drawer.

"Here. Let me help." He held up the tree while she got the purchased base ready.

"Slide it in."

He moved the tree into the base.

"Let me tighten it." She stood. "Done!" She stood away from the tree. "I forgot to buy a tree skirt. Actually, I packed something that might work." She went downstairs and returned with pink fabric draped over her arm. She spread it under the tree. "Not a real tree skirt, but a people skirt."

Jean-Marc laughed. Her creativity inspired him. What would she think of next?

"Now can I decorate it?" Henry stood with his eyes all aglow.

"Yes!" She snipped off the twine holding in the branches.

They fell outward with the scent of spruce.

"It's beautiful!" Henry grasped Livi's legs. "Thank

you, Livi!"

Memories of Jean-Marc's youth sprang up. He and his father would often get a live spruce and decorate it with pomanders. The entire apartment smelled of oranges and cloves. Or some years, they made stained-glass cookies and hung them on the tree next to the glass eggs from Poland.

Henry started with the chocolate ornaments. "We can eat these, right? On Christmas?"

"We'll see what your mom says."

Jean-Marc grabbed two glass bulbs and reached branches at the top. When he met Livi on the backside of the tree, he gulped at her closeness. "You're good at this kid stuff."

"Oh, thank you. This is just a temporary job." With a hint of a smile, she peeked around the tree.

Henry obsessed over the ornaments—picking them up by color, then by style, then by type.

"Temporary. What would you like to be?"

She winked. "A pastry chef, of course."

"I see. Why don't you? What's holding you back?" He would be happy to recommend her to several schools in Europe. He was close friends with instructors in London as well.

She strung tinsel from a bough above her. "I have a sister who is still in school."

"So?"

"I help pay her tuition." She shrugged. "We can't both be in school."

"Why not?"

Biting her lip, she hung more tinsel. "Private colleges are expensive." She bent to snag another ornament.

"Your mother isn't able to contribute?"

"My mom passed about four years ago." She stared at the ornament in her hands—a rocking horse with a red mane.

"I'm so sorry." He played with a string from a chocolate *Père Noël.* "I haven't seen my mother in years." Maybe he needed to drop by and visit her.

Lifting her head, she tilted her chin. "Why not?"

He shrugged and hung the ornament. "I don't know if she wants to see me."

"Of course she does. She's your mother."

He sighed. "Relationships aren't always easy. She left us. She doesn't want to hear from me."

She hung the rocking horse high on the tree. "Christmas is a great time to reach out. Does she live close by?"

He nodded. "Here in the *canton de* Fribourg."

Lowering her hand, she raised her eyebrows. "You should at least try to call her."

Huffing, he grinned. "I don't know." Mum caused him and Alexandre so much pain. And what would she say when he called? Would she be happy to hear from him? Or would she reject him again? His heart couldn't handle any more hurt.

"I would give anything to talk to my mother right now." Livi hung a chocolate ornament and stared at it. "You don't know what you have until it's gone, you know."

A spear of emotion lanced him like a hot sugar burn. He swallowed hard. "And you and your sister are close?"

Nodding, she reached above her head and hung a bulb. "The only reason I came with the Gordons for

Christmas was to help pay off part of her debt."

Leaning into the tree to hang a ball, he inhaled the sharp scent of the needles. "But surely she can earn her own way through university."

She bit her lip and lowered her eyebrows.

He wiped a few errant needles from his hands. "You are putting off your education and your dreams to help your sister. I don't understand."

She bent to retrieve another ornament, a Santa with a deer. "Wendy needs me. We need each other, because we only have each other."

"You are doing her a bear's favor by paying for her to go to school." Shaking his head, he dug into the bag for tinsel.

"A bear's favor?" She cocked her head.

He dripped tinsel on the boughs. "The phrase is a Polish idiomatic expression. It means you do something nice for someone, but the favor does more harm than good. She should learn to pay her own way. And you have genuine talent in the kitchen. You shouldn't let that go to waste."

Her face tinged pink.

Had he really complimented her? He couldn't remember the last compliment he gave to someone working in the kitchen. She wasn't equal to him in skill—indeed not. But she possessed a natural knack, an intuition that he envied. What took him years to learn, she already perfected. The silence wasn't awkward, but he realized he'd been thinking instead of talking. "What would you be doing if you weren't here in Switzerland?"

"Oh?" She raised her eyebrows. "Probably by this time I'd be back home in Indiana. And I'd be hanging out with my sister. She'd party at her college friends' houses, and I'd be watching your show learning how to perfect my craft."

Now he blushed. Heat rushed to his neck. "You deserve a better teacher." Perhaps he found someone he could work with after all.

Chapter 8

After two hours, the tree looked over-decorated. Ornaments, both glass and chocolate, hung from nearly every limb, and the whole thing looked like a 1970s disco party with all the lights and tinsel. Livi cleaned up the remaining ornaments.

In the kitchen, Jean-Marc rolled out the dough and cut out shapes.

His massive forearms worked the stiff texture easily. His prowess in the kitchen weakened her knees. She inhaled the scents of cinnamon and molasses and never wanted to forget this moment.

He carved a gingerbread man with large biceps. "This "cookie" is me!"

She shoved him with her shoulder. "Har, har!" He had large forearms, yes. But big biceps he did not have. "You might have a large ego, maybe."

"Want me to make one of you?"

Pushing back her hair, she shook her head. "No. I shudder to think what I would look like as a cookie." Her shoulders shook from laughter.

He held up a finger. "Ah, you don't trust my skills to make you as beautiful as you are."

The compliment sent thrills up her spine. "Oh, no. I trust your skills. I just don't think I'd look good as a cookie."

Holding his knife, he bent over the dough.

"Is that supposed to be me?" She pointed to a cookie with an enormous head. "You think I have a big head?"

He stuck out his tongue. "Wait and see." Grinning, he cut more cookies.

She slid them into the pre-heated oven. "Now we whip up the frosting."

"I'll do royal icing." He measured and sifted powdered sugar and meringue power. Then he added the smallest amount of water.

When the buzzer dinged, Livi jumped. When she opened the door, heat blasted her face.

After the cookies cooled, Jean-Marc filled a disposable bag and piped tiny curls on her head. "There, see? Beautiful."

Inside the gingerbread frame, he delicately recreated her curly hair, a smile, and even her outfit. His talent was indisputable. "The cookie does look like me, except for the blocky hands and large feet."

"Here. How about this?" He bent over his work and piped delicate hands and feet on the chunky cookie. "Better?"

She held it up. White, delicate piping swirled around the dark cookie. The contrast was stunning. "It's too pretty to eat." In fact, she planned to keep it forever.

He hovered close.

His eyes sparkled. Scents of ginger and vanilla clung to his shirt. A flash of desire washed over her. He snaked a warm hand around her back.

"We should've bought mistletoe."

His breath smelled of ginger. Her heart beat at a crazy fast pace. She gulped. "Who needs mistletoe?"

His lips brushed hers.

The mere touch sent goose bumps down her body. She leaned closer. His scent enticed her. She grasped his forearms.

He crushed her against him. His breath intensified.

Heat rushed all over. She needed to kiss him. She wrapped her arms up around his neck and stroked the silky strands of his hair.

A bolt of realization rocked her. She stepped back, shooting a glance to the couch. "Henry." She pointed to his little body across the cushions. Thank goodness Henry had fallen asleep on the couch. Relief filtered through her. If he saw them kissing and told his parents, that would be the end of her job.

Jean-Marc turned. "I'll carry him to his bed. Where's his room?"

"Follow me."

He easily lifted the sleeping boy and followed her downstairs.

The sight of Jean-Marc cradling Henry against his chest sent emotion straight to her heart. Compared to the heat of the kitchen, the basement dropped several degrees, cooling her. She needed a little cooling off after that kiss. She stood by his bedroom door and pointed.

He gently laid him into bed.

Livi removed his socks. "He can sleep in his clothes for one night." She closed the door behind her.

Jean-Marc stood close in the hall. He leaned a hand on the wood paneling. "Shall we continue?"

She lifted her chin. Tremors shook her. Now, instead of heat, chills ran through her body.

He raked a hand through her hair.

She lowered her chin. "Come see the rest of the

chalet." She needed a breather. Her mind whirred. What was she was doing? Where was this relationship going? She would only be here another week. Did he see her as a short-term fling?

At the pool room, she opened it. Humidity hit her in full force. She sat and pulled off her socks then stuck her feet in the water. The distraction was great.

He sat close and rolled up his pants over his bare feet. Shoulder to shoulder, they sat in the darkened pool room. The large, black window reflected the small lights illuminating the pool from below.

Livi kicked her feet, making small ripples in the water. "Thank you for the ride home and for sharing the Christmas chalets. I had a wonderful time."

"Meet me tomorrow night at my father's apartment for Christmas Eve? He'll be gone all night for Christmas Mass." He pulled his feet from the water. "I have a present for you."

"I have a present for you, too." Her heart rate kicked up a notch. When did he find time to buy her a present?

He wiped his feet on a towel. "We can exchange gifts."

Did he just ask her on date? She gulped. Nervous tremors raked through her. "I'm watching the kids until six." She tried to keep her voice as casual as possible. And she prayed the Gordons would spend Christmas Eve together as a family and not care if she left.

After tying on his shoes, he wrapped his arms around his legs. "All right. Can I pick you up around six-thirty?"

"Um, I'll meet you at your father's apartment." If the Gordons found out she had a man here, she'd be in big trouble—chastised at best—and fired at worst.

"All right. See you at six-thirty?" He raised his brows.

Gulping at his nearness, she nodded. "Sounds good."

He leaned over and kissed her cheek. "I'd better go." He reached down and squeezed her hand. "I'll see you tomorrow night." He stood and left by the downstairs door leading out to the yard.

She nodded, still dazed from his touch. Then an unsettling feeling boiled in the pit of her stomach.

On Christmas Eve, Livi wrapped her coat around her. What could she tell Mrs. Gordon when she asked her why Livi was leaving? Her heart thundered in her chest. She neared the door, hoping to slip away undetected.

"Where are you heading?"

Livi stopped and spun. Mrs. Gordon narrowed her beady eyes.

Both parents sat on the couch with ice packs on their knees. They skied earlier in the day, before the slopes closed at four.

Swallowing hard, she held her breath. She didn't want to lie. "Yves invited me to his house." Her face flamed hot. She most certainly would go to Yves's, but he invited her tomorrow. Small technicality.

"You okay going alone?" Mr. Gordon read something on his phone. "I can drive you."

He looked like he had little interest to get off the couch. "Switzerland is the safest country in the world. I'll be fine." She sidestepped the truth.

Looking up from his phone, Mr. Gordon furrowed his brow. "Just don't talk to any unsavory people." He rubbed his iced knees. "We're responsible for you. Be home by nine."

"Will do!" She opened the door and stepped out into the crunchy snow. Throughout the town of Moleson, snow piled near the other chalets. Thankfully, the Swiss maintenance crews salted and scraped the steep roads, or she would've slipped while walking down to the bus stop. The sky turned midnight blue. The contrast with the snowy, peaked roofs amazed her. Livi shivered. She was in Switzerland. The streetlights cast a yellow tint on the snow.

She caught the bus. The forty-five-minute descent seemed to take forever. The light below drew closer and closer. At last, the bus dropped her off. She hiked the rest of the way to his house.

Cold breezes swept through her. Christmas lights hung across the streets in the shape of a star. The whole atmosphere spoke Christmas, and a pang of longing swept through her. What was Wendy doing Christmas Eve? Was she all alone? Maybe she should call her later. She checked her phone. Indiana was in the middle of the night now.

She checked the time. She'd arrive a few minutes early. A thrill went through her stomach. She replayed her memories in the kitchen of baking with Jean-Marc. A smile stole across her lips. Their kiss. She touched her lips with her hand. Would she get more kisses tonight? She shivered, and not from the cold.

****

The Eglise de Notre-Dame Cathedral chimed six-thirty. Jean-Marc placed the finishing touches on his Christmas tree *croquembouche*. It stood nearly half a meter high with over a hundred mini pastries stuck to a cone. Spun sugar covered the top of the green-iced *choux* pastry. A cookie star perched on top. He woke before four a.m. to prepare for her coming tonight, baking his best for her. He worked without resting until now. Livi brought out a side in him he hadn't seen in ages—a fervor and passion to create he had while he was younger. A renewed zest for baking pumped through him. He made the laborious *marrons glacées* and also a *bûche de Nöel*. At the end of the afternoon, he recreated her peppermint *macaron* recipe, using his method, not hers.

Tonight was the night. He was sure she was the one who could help him with his show. Just being with her in the kitchen exhilarated him. Cooking gingerbread in her chalet kitchen was the highlight of the last few years—a light in the darkness.

At six-thirty-two, a knock sounded at the door.

He flew to answer it.

Livi stood on the doorstep. She straightened her curly hair. A wrapped package glistened between her gloved hands.

"*Entre!*" He swept a hand before her.

"What smells amazing in here?" She swept back her hair and stepped inside. "Did you make all this?"

He nodded, then scowled. "I probably should've made dinner. Have you eaten?"

"It's Christmas Eve." She set down the gift on the coffee table. "We can eat cake for dinner."

He helped her off with her coat. "Indeed!" In the kitchen, he sliced a piece of the yule log and slipped it on a decorative plate.

She dug in her fork. "Oh, my gosh. This is amazing!" With each bite, her eyes lit brighter. "You know, I was watching your video on the *bûche de Noël* before coming here. In fact, you had an announcement. I never got to hear it. What was it?"

"Something I want to talk to you about. Come sit." He beckoned her to sit alongside him on the couch. His father hung a sprig of mistletoe over the window where the couch rested. He thought about nestling it into the *bûche de Nöel*. Yet, he honored the tradition of putting nothing inedible in with food.

"Is that mistletoe?" She raised her gaze to look before sitting.

Lifting a brow, he slid his arm along the backside of the couch. "Maybe."

She set her plate on the coffee table and settled into the cushions.

He rested his hand over hers, running a thumb over her knuckles.

Furrowing her eyebrows, she clasped it. "What is it?"

"I have a question for you." His heart felt like a mixer on high speed.

"Okay."

He inhaled, mustering all his courage. "At the end of the month, I start a new contract with a London producer, taping new shows for international streaming."

She smiled and held his hand tighter. "How very exciting!"

"One thing. The producer gave me a deadline to find a partner to work the show in two days, or he'll cancel my show."

"Sounds doable." She nodded. "I'm sure lots of people would love to work with you."

"That's the problem." He exhaled. The truth he didn't want exposed haunted him. "Not many do."

She tilted her head. "Why not?"

He gulped. Sharing this part of his story required baring all his soul. He'd never spoken of this experience to anyone, not even his father. He took a deep breath and, releasing her hands, stood. "Years ago, when I first started recording my own videos, I worked with a woman named Penelope."

She raised her eyebrows. "Okay."

So far, his narrative sounded bad, but he had to explain everything so she'd understand this part of his life. He paced in front of the couch. "We worked together, and we formed a romantic attachment."

Livi shifted.

Jean-Marc gulped again. Tremors raked through him. Would she still stay after she heard his story? "She was excellent in the kitchen, and we made a great team. But then, after we spent months baking, she stole the recipes we'd created together and started her own show." His tongue went dry. All these years, and Penelope still hurt him. "She said she just used me to get to my creative genius."

"Oh, Jean-Marc." Livi stood and wrapped her arms around him.

Her warmth gave him the courage to continue. "So after our painful separation, I refused to trust anyone. I was so suspicious of anyone who wanted to be with me because she might to steal my livelihood. I struggled to find a partner who was worthy of my talents and my trust—until I met you."

Livi took a sharp intake of breath.

He pushed her out of the embrace so he could see

her face. "You have inspired me to do my best." His heart opened. The confession both relieved him and scared him. "I was in a rut until I met you. You didn't take my attitude, and you wouldn't let me bully you in the kitchen. You are truly my equal."

She leaned in and kissed him.

He crashed on her lips in desperation and hunger. He cupped her chin, drew her closer, and savored each breath they shared. She smelled of chocolate and sugar, but even without the cake, she always tasted sweet.

She broke away. "So, what's the question?"

"Pardon? Oh, I return to London the day after Christmas to start filming. And I wondered if you would come with me." His invitation hung in the air. He gulped. What would she say?

Chapter 9

Standing, Livi gasped for air. With one question, he just asked her to change the trajectory of her life. She brushed a hand over her forehead. Heat from her sweater overwhelmed her. She needed air. Her knees gave out. She sat. He offered her a chance of a lifetime—a dream fulfilled. But what about Henry and Alice? She couldn't just leave them. "When do you start filming?"

"In two days."

His words tore at her heart. "You want me to give up my steady job in two days? And move to London, one of the most expensive cities in the world? I don't know what to say."

He held out his hands. "You don't have to agree now. Think about my proposal, and let me know when you're ready."

Heat rushed to her face. What about Wendy? Moving would be expensive. Changing her life was costly. Would she still afford to pay Wendy's tuition? And what about applying for a work visa? Shipping her few belongings overseas would cost a fortune. "What would the salary be?"

He cleared his throat. "I'm not sure."

Her heart thundered. "I can't do that." She almost whispered her response. How could he ask her to change her life so quickly?

"What?" He lowered his brow. "Why not? Didn't you want to learn how to cook pastry? This arrangement would be brilliant. We could have contests on the show. Who creates a better pastry, me or the amateur?" He grinned. "Or I could teach you as we go along."

Her cheeks flamed as if he'd slapped her. She stood. With narrowed eyes, she jabbed the air. "You still don't think I'm good enough for you."

He jumped back. "No, that's not what I meant at all. This is an incredible opportunity. I like you. We work well together. You can stop putting your life on hold and start doing what you've dreamed."

"What do you know of my dreams?" She thrust a hand to her chest. "I have to take care of people. I can't just drop them like that." Alice and Henry…She imagined their little crestfallen faces if she left. She paced, focusing on the carpet.

Jean-Marc huffed. "Are you referring to your sister? Tell her to get a job and pay her own way through school."

She snapped up her head. "My sister needs me."

He wagged a finger. "No. You need to be needed. Why can't you stand up for yourself? Because you have a hero complex. You have to be the savior. Do something for yourself for once."

Energy flew through her. "How dare you!" She snatched her coat. Tears stung her eyes. "And be selfish, like you?" She gulped. "What about you? You don't keep people around because you have abandonment issues. Your mother left you, and you think every woman will leave you, and so you dump them first. Is that right?" Her hands shook.

Jean-Marc widened his eyes. He dropped his jaw.

Her words hit their mark. She instantly regretted them. Folding her coat, she tucked it into the crook of her elbow. "You know what? This whole thing was a bad idea. We're done." Somehow in her raging pulse and blurred eyesight, she found the doorknob. She flew through the door. Her footsteps echoed on the concrete as she thundered down the stairs.

"Livi."

Jean-Marc's voice reverberated down the three floors.

She didn't care. How could he accuse her so harshly? A wound dug into her heart. She found the front door and opened it to the chilly wind. She crunched along the snow to the bus stop and waited. *Wait*. She read the timetable for holidays. The bus had a different schedule on Christmas Eve. *Great*. She plopped onto the bench. The bus wouldn't arrive for another forty-five minutes.

Where would she even go? She didn't want to go home to the Gordons' chalet. They were having family time, and she would feel awkward being with them. She opened her phone and dialed the only other person who would be lonely on Christmas Eve—Wendy. Thankfully, before coming to Europe she upgraded her mobile phone data to include calling from Europe.

Ring. Ring. Ring.

The tone sounded loud as a foghorn in her ear.

No answer. No wonder. The time in Indiana was early afternoon.

She checked the schedule again. The bus still had another forty minutes. *Fine*. Zipping up her jacket, she shrugged against the wind. She'd just walk home. In the dark. On slippery roadsides.

Except for the porch light, the chalet was dark when she reached the mountain top. Buses didn't run often on the holiday schedule, and it was past nine when she kicked the snow from her frozen toes at the front door. Unlocking the door with her key, she creaked open the door to the dim lights inside. At nine-thirty, the kids were already in bed. Heat warmed her. She shed her jacket.

Mr. and Mrs. Gordon sat on the couch near the fireplace.

"Livi, will you come in here? We need to talk." Mrs. Gordon rose and stood by the fireplace.

That tone! Livi's heart lunged. She knew she was late. She'd have to explain that the buses ran less frequently, and she certainly couldn't get a ride home with Jean-Marc after their fight. She stepped into the living area. The somber attitude contrasted so sharply with the brightly colored presents and the lights from the tree.

A crease marred Mrs. Gordon's forehead.

"Henry told me something disturbing as I tucked him into bed tonight."

Livi's heart thundered. Who knew what secrets he shared?

"He said you had a man over here?" She crossed her arms over her cashmere sweater.

Ice washed through Livi. "I—someone helped bring in the Christmas tree." Guilty heat boiled in her stomach.

Mrs. Gordon cocked her head. "Henry said he stayed and decorated cookies."

Ache weighed in her chest. Their recent fight now

soiled those sweet memories. "Yes, he did."

Taking a deep breath, Mrs. Gordon lowered her chin. "Livi, you know how we feel about having boyfriends in the house."

"All we did was decorate the tree and make cookies." The words exploded from her mouth. The injustice of her accusations raked through her. Oh, the irony! She was getting in trouble for having a guy over on the night they broke up. She shook her head.

Mr. Gordon leaned forward from his spot on the couch. "You violated your contract."

"I'm afraid this leads to a termination." Mrs. Gordon drew her lips to a straight line.

Heat rose to her chest. "No—I'm really sorry. He's not a boyfriend. He was a mutual friend—"

Shaking her head, Mrs. Gordon held out a hand. "Who he is doesn't matter. He's a distraction and cause for a release. We'll allow you to stay the rest of the week, but then we'll be searching for a new nanny when we return to Boston."

Tears stung Livi's eyes. "I promise it won't happen again. Please, can I stay?" All she could think of was little Henry's face—the sadness in his eyes.

Mrs. Gordon stepped forward. "Rules are rules, and they cannot be broken. We have enjoyed you as our nanny, but having a boyfriend over while you're on the clock is one thing we will not tolerate."

A weight settled on Livi. She nodded, then lowered her head. She dragged her feet downstairs, away from their penetrating gazes. Collapsing on her bed, she finally let herself cry. Her shoulders heaved. Fired from her job for a guy who didn't even think she was good enough to cook with him and who accused her of needing to be needed. What a jerk! She curled into her pillow.

She squeezed her face against the pain gathering in the back of her neck. She'd have to find a job when she returned. What could she do? On Christmas Eve—the happiest of all nights, she couldn't sleep. Pain swallowed her whole. She would never be happy again.

****

The sun peeked into Livi's room, reflecting off the snow of her ground level room. She opened her eyes. Christmas Day dawned bright and clear. At the smell of nervous sweat, she turned up her nose. She still wore her clothes from last night. The taste of stale chocolate cake washed over her teeth. Ugh.

The cows stared from their black paintings on the wall. She tossed the covers over her head. Movement from upstairs—a bit of Henry's laughter, Alice's wail, and Mr. Gordon's heavy footsteps—turned her stomach.

She laid her head on the pillow. Her eyes ached from crying. She couldn't face the Gordons. How awkward it would be. But she couldn't stay in bed all day. She was about to suffocate. Where could she go? Every store in Switzerland was closed today. If only she had family here... *Wait.*

Earlier, Yves invited her over. She gulped. Hope sprang up through her. She jumped out of bed, changed her clothes, washed her face, and padded up the stairs with her coat and purse.

In the living room, the Gordons opened presents, laughing and thanking each other.

She opened the front door to a rush of fresh alpine wind, hoping to slip out without any awkward confrontations. Just as she was about to close the wooden door behind her, she saw little Henry's hand slip through the jamb.

His face appeared in the small space between the wood and the frame. He swung open the door. "Where are you going? You haven't opened my present."

Her heart caught in her chest. She swallowed hard. His pajamas were too thin for this cold. How could she tell him the truth? "I am visiting my family."

A grin lit up his face. "I can't wait for you to come back. I want to show you what Santa brought. We can play with it all year!"

Pain constricted her chest. She didn't have the heart to tell him, but maybe telling him now was better than later. She found her zipper. "Listen, Henry, I won't be staying long after we get home."

He cocked his head. "Why not?"

She gulped. She couldn't tell him why Mrs. Gordon fired her. "I have to go away, and you get a new nanny."

Mrs. Gordon appeared at the door in her pajamas— a matching mauve robe and bottoms.

Henry leaned forward. "I didn't tell her we ate so much sugar."

"I know." A lump formed in her throat. "You're a good boy, Henry." She tousled his hair. "When I go, we'll stay friends. Don't worry."

"I don't want you to leave." Tears welled in his eyes. "You're my only friend."

She wasn't sure if he meant for her to stay now or later. Either way, his words churned in her heart. Kneeling, she faced him, eye to eye. "You're a big boy, and soon you'll go to kindergarten, and you'll make lots of friends."

"Come, Henry. You still have more presents." Mrs. Gordon wrapped her robe around her more tightly.

"I don't want presents. I want Livi." He threw his arms around her.

Livi squeezed her eyes shut and hugged him so tight. She loved feeling his little arms around her. Then she let go. "Henry, you need to go. Your mother needs you." Livi pried his arms off her. "I have to go to my cousin's house. You remember Yves. We met him at the party. I haven't seen him in a long time, and I want to talk with him."

"Isn't that where you went last night?" Mrs. Gordon narrowed her eyes. "Or did you lie about that, too?"

With conviction blasting heat to her face, Livi lowered her head again to Henry. She brushed the hair out of his big brown eyes. "I need to go." She tore herself away and nearly slid on the slush beneath her feet. She wasn't sure where she was going. Right now, she just needed to leave.

"Go inside, Henry." Mrs. Gordon patted the back of Henry's head. She wrapped her robe around her and cocked a hip. "You're lucky we don't sue you for your breach of contract."

Livi faced Mrs. Gordon. Her nose turned red and blotchy in the cold. Her hair hung in stringy tendrils, not at all like her usual shellacked coif. At that moment, Livi broke. "No. You can't mistreat me anymore. You didn't fulfill your end of the contract. More than once, you asked me to watch the kids on my days off. I have proof that you didn't fulfill your end of the bargain. You should be lucky I don't sue you." Livi jabbed a finger in her direction. A bit of power rushed through her.

Mrs. Gordon shrank inside her robe. "I see. I hope you will still finish out your contract for the rest of the stay, including the flight home."

"Right now, I'm not sure I will. I need a break after caring for the kids almost non-stop since I've been here. And I want to spend time with my cousin since I didn't get a chance to talk to him because I watched the kids at his engagement party." Livi turned on her heel and marched downhill toward the valley. She hoped she projected more confidence than what she felt because really she didn't know what she would do if she didn't go home with the Gordons. She couldn't stay in Switzerland. Imagining Mr. and Mrs. Gordon fighting over who had to pace up and down the aisles with Alice and take Henry to the bathroom a bazillion times eased a bit of the ache in her heart. She laughed out loud, a quick, terse laugh. Would they all four be in coach? She huffed. Somehow, she doubted it.

But misery overtook her again. She yelled at Jean-Marc last night. Would she ever be able to fix it? Or was their relationship just not meant to be? After traveling down the mountain, away from the chalet, she dialed Yves's number. "I need a ride. I can't explain. Can you pick me up?"

"Stay where you are. I'll come."

After sending him her location, she collapsed into a snow pile. Fresh tears stung her eyes. A little voice told her that when she felt sorry for herself, she should do something for someone else. Well, she couldn't do much for anyone while she sat atop a mountain in Switzerland.

She should call Wendy. Was she alone on Christmas Eve, missing Livi? She unlocked her phone and dialed her number. Music blasted into her ear. "Wendy? Are you there?"

"Hello?"

"Where are you, and what are you doing?" Why did Wendy blast non-holiday music on Christmas Eve?

"Sorry. With so much noise, I can't hear you." Wendy shouted into the phone.

"Where are you?"

"I'll go into my room where it's quieter. Ew, what are you doing in here?"

The door slammed.

"Get out." Muffled sounds. "You still there, Liv? Sorry. These people were in my room. Okay, Merry Christmas! Are you still in Switzerland?"

"Yes. What is going on?" Her stomach turned.

"A bunch of my friends couldn't make it home for Christmas because of this big blizzard, so we threw a party here."

A thread of annoyance laced through Livi. Wendy couldn't pay her own credit card bill but had enough money to host a party? "Okay." She checked the time. "Well, I just called to see how you're doing. I didn't want you to be alone."

"You are so sweet. You really are the best sister. But as you can hear, I'm not alone. In fact, I should probably get back to my party. I don't want to be a poor hostess."

Livi bit her lip. Her entire world fell apart, and Wendy worried about offending her friends? She hadn't exactly told Wendy she was having a crisis, but still!

"Oh, and because my grades slipped this last

semester, I lost my scholarship, so now you'll have to pay full tuition in January. I wanted to wait until you got back from your trip, but since you're on the phone...and don't forget, Livi, rent is due by the first."

Heat spurred through her. Livi gripped the phone. Didn't Jean-Marc suggest Livi needed to stop doing her a bear's favor? "You know what?" She gulped. Courage anchored her, spread through her like fire. "You get a job and pay your own tuition and rent." Her voice barely squeaked out. Telling off Mrs. Gordon was one thing. Standing up to Wendy—her best, her only sister—was another.

"What?"

Sitting up, Livi drew a strengthening breath. "I'm not paying your rent next month. Or your credit card bill or your tuition. If you have time to host a party, you can get a job." Her resolve hardened.

"But Livi, I have to focus on my schooling. I can't work."

Truth flowed through her. Livi should've said these words years ago. "You didn't focus enough to keep your scholarship. Pay for your last semester yourself. I'm done, Wendy. I'm done being your ATM, your bank, and your, your patsy. I'm not paying for anything else."

"But if I don't have the money, I get kicked out of school."

Livi thrust up her chin. A surge of power flowed through her. Mom would've wanted to her to cut her loose. "So be it. You can take out loans or get a job like everyone else."

"What happened in Switzerland that made you so mean?"

Huffing, Livi switched ears. "Mean? You've walked all over me for the last three and a half years—since Mom died! Gad! I've put off my dreams and worked a job with zero appreciation to pay for your life. You want to know what happened in Switzerland? I found myself, and I don't want to be the savior."

Wendy hung up.

Leaning back into the snow, Livi shook her head. Resolution surged through her body. She wasn't being mean. She stood up for herself. Wendy had taken advantage of her long enough.

Still, emptiness threaded through her. With Wendy mad at her, with her relationship with Jean-Marc over, the Gordons threatening to sue her, she had nowhere to go.

A steel gray sports car crunched in the snow drift. The tinted window lowered.

Yves removed his sunglasses. He flashed a smile. "Merry Christmas, Livi."

Gratitude welled in her heart. She jumped up from the snow. Upon seeing him, tears leaked from her eyes. Bursting with relief, she opened the door, brushing snow from her bottom. "Oh, Yves, I've really messed up, and I don't know what to do."

"We'll take you to Lainey. She can fix anything." He shifted his car into gear and rolled down the snowy streets.

Could Lainey help her fix a broken relationship?

Chapter 10

Jean-Marc woke to butter and flour scents wafting in. Sounds of pots and pans clinking in the kitchen brought back so many childhood memories. His father now baked in the kitchen. Even on Christmas morning, even after a late night of church, his father sacrificed and arose early to treat Jean-Marc. Pulling on clothes, he slipped into the kitchen to help.

"How was Midnight Mass?" He popped a bite of *crêpe* into his mouth. Buttery flavors melted on his tongue.

"Wonderful!" With his meaty arms, Alexandre Dobrinsky swirled *crêpe* batter around a small pan. A stack already grew on a plate near the stove. Three *crêpes*, folded into quarters with banana-nut sauce drizzled on top, lay on a plate.

"For me?" Jean-Marc inhaled deeply, breathing in the scents of caramel.

Alexandre nodded. "You should have come with me to church."

Exhaling, Jean-Marc slouched against the counter, holding the plate against his chest. "I had a date." Some date. He shook his head. What went wrong? How had he misjudged her feelings? Her pained expression wounded him. And now he was out of time. He flew to London tomorrow. He stuffed a forkful in his mouth. Mmmmm. Caramel glaze, bananas, and pecans smothered his tongue. His father was an artist and a taste magician. Jean-Marc almost forgot his heartache.

"Oh, how is Livi?" His father smiled.

With his father's words, his heartache returned. He finished his bite and licked a bit of caramel dripped on his finger. "Mad."

Alexandre lowered the pan. "What happened?"

Jean-Marc's chest ached. He couldn't find the words. She insulted him to his core. He didn't have attachment issues. Stuffing his hands into his pockets, he shrugged. "Our relationship is over."

Alexandre moved the *crêpe* pan off the gas and turned off the burner. "Oh, I'm so sorry."

Sighing, Jean-Marc swiped a hand down his face. "I don't want to talk about it. Anyway, these banana-nut *crêpes* are amazing. You've outdone yourself."

"Thank you."

After breakfast, Jean-Marc opened his present from his father—an expensive dough press he'd wanted. "Thank you! It's perfect. I'll use it often."

Alexandre opened his present from Jean-Marc. "Oh, a new butane torch. You knew mine was getting old. You're so sweet to remember."

"I didn't want you setting the house on fire with that old one."

Alexandre leaned forward and patted Jean-Marc's cheek. "Thank you. I'm so glad you followed in my footsteps."

One present remained under the tree—Livi's gift. Jean-Marc's stomach churned. Perhaps he could find another girl named Livi and give her his signed copy of his latest book. Shaking his head, he stood, went to the kitchen, and opened the fridge. The *bûche de Noël* sat on the shelf. Reminders of her were everywhere. He picked up the platter and tossed the cake in the trash. He felt his father's gaze. Wasting cake was not something that happened often in this family.

As Alexandre inhaled, his chest expanded like risen dough. He wasn't happy. Jean-Marc could tell.

Alexandre's gaze focused on something in the distance. "You know. I always wished I had apologized to your mother. I was so stubborn. But alas, I wanted her to apologize to me. My pride was a wedge in our relationship." He dropped his gaze to Jean-Marc. "I don't want the same misunderstanding to happen to you."

His mother. Neither Alexandre nor Jean-Marc had spoken of her in a while. Memories of Christmas mornings with his mother, curled up with her *papillon* dog, Fritz, flooded him. His mother always allowed him to open his presents first before anyone else. She wrapped her arms around him and encouraged him to slow down and savor the moment. An ache rose in his heart.

When Jean-Marc and Livi decorated the tree, she said she would give anything to talk to her mother. He had the opportunity. Why waste it? He should stop putting it off. "I'm calling Mum."

Alexandre opened his mouth and closed it again.

"I want to wish her Merry Christmas." Jean-Marc dialed her number. When the phone picked up, he swallowed hard. His hands trembled. "Hello, Mother. Merry Christmas!" His voice caught.

"Jean-Marc?"

The surprise in her voice flamed his cheeks. He shouldn't allow calling his own mother to be such a rare event. "How are you doing?"

"You haven't called in a long time."

Now her voice turned slightly accusing. But she was right. A hot wave of guilt flashed through his chest. He brushed his hair back. "I'm here in Switzerland with Dad."

Alexandre dropped his head to his chest.

"He wanted me to tell you he is sorry." Facing Alexandre, Jean-Marc grinned.

Alexandre's head shot up. His face reddened. "What are you doing?"

His eyes bugged out. Jean-Marc laughed at his shaking head.

"I didn't mean for you to tell her!"

Silence lengthened on the other end of the phone.

Jean-Marc counted to ten.

"Thank you for telling me." Her voice trembled.

"I love you, Mum." He held his breath. His heart nearly burst from his chest. Years of pain eased in his chest. It wasn't gone, but calling her was a great first step. "I was wondering if I could visit you sometime. Maybe later today?"

Her breath caught. "You are always welcome here. I love you, too, son."

Warmth flooded his heart. Tears pricked at his eyes. All those years he never called. He was too afraid of the pain. "I'll text you before I come." Speaking around the lump in his throat proved difficult. He hung up before he blubbered.

An immense weight lifted off his chest. She didn't reject him. Maybe Livi was right. Maybe he pushed away people. Did he push away Livi? He needed to find her. He snatched his jacket, his phone, and a plate of the peppermint *macarons*.

****

All the way up the mountain, Livi told Yves what happened. The words poured out.

But he didn't say much in return. He stopped at a house high in the mountains.

He couldn't live up here. This was probably his mother's house. Where else would he be on Christmas?

Yves parked his car in the garage and opened the car door.

When she entered the two-story house, Livi felt heat envelop her. Wooden stairs led to the kitchen, which smelled of spices and cream. Her stomach growled. She had eaten little in the last twenty-four hours, only a bite or two of chocolate *roulade*.

"Livi!" Lainey, dressed in a different Christmas sweater, bounded across the polished wood floor.

"Lainey." Livi embraced her. With this act of sheer love, tears sprang to her eyes. "I'm having a horrible Christmas."

Lainey pulled away and brushed hair out of Livi's face. "What's wrong?"

"Everything, everything!" She hated to sound so dramatic.

Lainey led her over to a wooden breakfast nook bench.

Removing her coat, Livi sat on the hard wood. "Jean-Marc and I fought last night." She left off the violation of contract and the discussion with Wendy this morning. For some reason, she focused on Jean-Marc. Maybe because she would never see him again. Or their relationship was the one thing she couldn't repair. She told Lainey all about the offer to join his show, to move to London, and to quit her life in Boston—all in two days. She explained how she rejected his offer and left in a huff. Of course, she didn't share the part where he accused her of needing to be needed. A lump formed in her throat.

Yves fetched a tissue but stayed amazingly out of the way. In fact, he texted someone on his phone and wasn't even paying attention. Rude! Livi blew her hot nose. "I've messed up with Jean-Marc, and I cannot fix it."

"Posh, why do you say that?" Lainey patted her hand.

"I insulted him." Livi grasped her fingers. In the living room, a giant Christmas tree nearly swept the thirty-foot ceiling. A few presents remained under the tree. *Great!* And she ruined their Christmas morning.

"So?" Lainey shrugged.

Livi folded the tissue. "Why would he forgive me? Why would he give me a second chance? He could get another partner just like that." She snapped her fingers. "What do I offer? Nothing."

Lainey released her hand and pushed over a box of chocolate. "You have more than you think. You are creative and kind. Don't let him walk all over you. You are the one person who treats him as a person instead of someone famous. And sometimes treating him as a friend means you have to say the ugly truth."

Huffing, Livi snagged a chocolate and bit into the piece. "But I don't know how to fix our relationship. It's broken beyond repair."

"Nothing is beyond repair." Lainey inhaled. She gripped Livi's hand. "You know I'm opening my new chocolate boutique next year, right?"

"That's exciting." What a weird thing to bring up right now.

Lainey's eyes lit up. "I've been testing and making chocolates this entire month. You know how finicky chocolate is, right?"

Sniffling, Livi nodded. She worked with chocolate enough to know she never wanted to be a chocolatier.

"Tempering can be a bear."

"Indeed." How many times had Livi burned the chocolate or mis-tempered it, and the chalky bloom formed on her lovely creations.

Lainey brushed back her honey-brown hair. "Well, I made a batch, and my chocolate wouldn't temper."

After sniffing into her tissue, Livi grabbed another chocolate and savored the earthly aroma. "Why are we talking about chocolate?"

Pocketing his phone, Yves stepped closer. "Because to Lainey, love equals chocolate."

Lainey rolled her eyes. "I have a point. Just listen. When you mis-temper chocolate, and it doesn't form a beautiful shine or a nice crack on the first go, what do you do?"

Shaking her head, Livi shrugged. She knew a lot about chocolate, but not how to troubleshoot when things went wrong. "Throw it all away?" Such a waste!

Lainey shook her head. "You chop up more chocolate—fresh chocolate—and add it to the mis-tempered chocolate."

Livi dropped her jaw. "But why?"

Leaning closer, Lainey licked her lips. "The new chocolate helps re-crystalize the mis-tempered chocolate. The good chocolate kind of tells the mis-tempered chocolate, 'Hey, get into form.' That's what

you need to do with your friendship with Jean-Marc.
You can't just throw away a relationship because you
fought. Guess what!" She glanced toward Yves and
then back at Livi. "You will fight. You will have
disagreements. And you will not always be your best."
She emphasized each sentence with a nod of her head.
Sitting back, she gestured with her hands. "You've just
mis-tempered your relationship. Throw in more good
memories, more good vibes, better communication, add
a dash of forgiveness, a sprinkle of humility, and a
teaspoon of humor—okay, maybe I've taken this
analogy too far. Anyway, you will solidify your
relationship again. This one fight is not the end of the
world."

Livi sniffed. She glanced from Lainey to Yves.
"What would you do if someone asked you to leave
your country and start a new life doing something you
love? Would you do it, even if change scared you do
death?"

Yves moved to Lainey and rubbed her shoulder.

Smiling up at Yves, she grabbed his hand and held
it to her heart. "Yes. I left my country, and I found
something I love more than chocolate. I'm never letting
go of either." She dropped his hand and leaned forward
to grab Livi's. "Now, go find Jean-Marc. Tell him how
you feel. Let the apology re-temper your relationship."

A knock sounded on the front door.

Heads turned in unison.

"How unexpected!" Lainey crossed to the door.
"Who would visit Christmas morning?"

"I sent a well-timed text." Yves beat her to the
foyer.

Livi heard his voice before he she saw Jean-Marc.

Emotion shot energy through her. Was he still mad? The men spoke in French, and so she didn't understand the conversation.

With a smile, Lainey turned. "Livi."

Blinking back tears, Livi rose.

Jean-Marc stepped inside. He wore a dark shirt with his sleeves pushed up to three-quarters. In his hand hung his coat. He tossed it aside. "Please accept my apology. I should have been more tactful in my proposal. I shouldn't have put so much pressure on you."

Livi's heart melted. She swelled like a *soufflé*. "I was shocked. I didn't know how to handle it all. You were right about everything. I called my sister and told her she could take care of her own bills this semester. I even told my bosses they were lucky I didn't sue for breach of contract."

Jean-Marc's eyebrows rose. "My! You are making strides." He took her hand. "And I have made some changes, too. I thought about what you said about wishing you could talk to your mom. I called my mother. She wants to meet this afternoon and talk. Would you like to come and meet her?"

Warmth flooded Livi. He listened. "I would love to meet her." Maybe Christmas wouldn't be so bad after all.

"Wonderful!" He tilted down his chin and lifted his brows. "Would you come to London with me? Would you be willing to change jobs and leave everything? You don't have to come tomorrow. I can tell my producers—"

"Hush." She placed a finger on his perfect lips. "If I come, I don't come to only help you or to follow you.

I come because I want to see where our relationship can go. I'll come because the cooking show is a great opportunity for me, too. Let's see what we can make together." Thrills sent chills down her spine. London! Television. "However, I don't feel—enough. I'm scared."

"We'll be together every step of the way." He opened her hand and kissed her palm.

Warmth spread through her. "Look, mistletoe." She glanced up to a sprig of green hanging from the ceiling.

"*J'en profit.*" He bent, holding her around her waist, and kissed her. "We must use it!"

Livi fell into his embrace. The warmth of his touch calmed her and excited her all at once. Leaning into him, she inhaled the scent of caramels and banana. "I hope we will always make sweet things together."

"Are you talking metaphorically now?" Jean-Marc slipped a hand up her cheek.

His tender brush of his hand sent chills down her spine. "Maybe. And if we ever fight again, I hope we can re-temper our relationship like this."

"Sounds like a chocolate analogy." He grinned. "I love a good baking comparison."

She kissed his unshaven cheek. An idea lit into her mind. "Chocolate-mint macarons. Or maybe chocolate s'mores!"

He bent and brushed his lips against hers. "If kissing gives you more baking ideas, I must kiss you often."

"I'll welcome that suggestion." She stroked his cheek, feeling the warmth of his face. "Then we will work beautifully in the kitchen, together."

Epilogue

Six months later...

Livi held her breath as she turned on the TV in her London flat. Since Christmas, she relocated and applied for a Temporary Worker's Creative Visa. The producers signed a certificate of sponsorship, guaranteeing her the salary, helped her find a great location, and even subsidized part of her rent.

Their show, *Patisseries and Passion*, aired the last episode of the season today. She shook her head. The last six months had been a crazy whirlwind of change. And not all the change was smooth sailing. The learning curve was steep, but Jean-Marc had been there the whole time, right by her side. Plus, saying goodbye to Boston, particularly the Gordons, was difficult. She didn't fly home with them from Switzerland. When she went to retrieve her baking stuff—the only physical things she cared about—she was greeted by Mrs. Gordon coolly.

She bagged Livi's pans and equipment and had it all waiting by the front door. Mrs. Gordon wouldn't allow her to see the kids.

Livi sneaked a note for Henry to the new nanny behind Mrs. Gordon's back. Livi wasn't sure who she felt the most sorry for—the new nanny or the kids. Alice and Henry would always hold a place in her heart. Livi hoped Henry would remember her.

At the beginning of January, Wendy called and begged for tuition money.

Livi caved and gave her half on the condition of repayment.

Jean-Marc shook his head all through the phone call.

But what did Livi care about a few thousand dollars now? She focused more on her promising future. So far, the show was a success. Early on, someone in the biz warned her to avoid reading the reviews, but she couldn't help sneaking a peek. Most were positive. She picked up the latest copy of *London Gazette* and read reviews:

The chemistry is palpable between Jean-Marc and Livi.

Where has this show been all my life?

Aren't these two adorable? Their flirting has to be real.

I love how Livi sometimes outdoes Jean-Marc, and he takes it like a champ. So much better than his last show.

Jean-Marc entered her living room with a plate of chocolate-orange *macarons* and two drinks. "Don't forget. We sign the merchandising deals this weekend."

"Who could forget?" The negotiations had been lengthy—the contracts long and tedious. But to see her own products in stores would be so, so worth it. She bit into the chocolate-orange *macaron*. "You know these aren't that bad."

"Yours are just better." He handed her a glass. "To your success."

She cuddled into his chest. "No, to our success."

"Indeed." They clinked glasses. He leaned in and

placed a kiss on her lips.

When the kiss ended, Livi sipped the fizzy bubbles. Gratitude filled her heart for *macarons*, for self-assurance, and for Jean-Marc—all of those things led her to where she was today. She would never forget it all started with a bit of mistletoe and *macarons*.

A word about the author...

Amey Zeigler received her B.A. in Communication from University of Arizona. When she was nine years old, she started writing romantic mysteries and has been obsessed with the genre ever since. The Swiss Mishap won third place in the OCCRWA's Book Buyer's Best Contest for Contemporary Romance. While attending university, she put her studies on hold to live in France and Switzerland for a year and a half. She lives with her husband and three children near Austin, Texas. http://www.ameyzeigler.com

Other Titles by the Author
August Blues
Baker's Dozen
Summer of Sundaes
The Swiss Mishap

Thank you for purchasing
this publication of The Wild Rose Press, Inc.

For questions or more information
contact us at
info@thewildrosepress.com.

The Wild Rose Press, Inc.
www.thewildrosepress.com